USA TODAY BESTSELLING AUTHOR

Dale Mayer

MOUNTAIN 08

SHADOW RECON

MOUNTAIN: SHADOW RECON, BOOK 8
Beverly Dale Mayer
Valley Publishing Ltd.

Copyright © 2024

ISBN-13: 978-1-778862-69-4
Print Edition

Books in This Series:

Magnus, Book 1

Rogan, Book 2

Egan, Book 3

Barret, Book 4

Whalen, Book 5

Nikolai, Book 6

Teegan, Book 7

Mountain, Book 8

About This Book

Deep in the permafrost of the Arctic, a joint task force, comprised of over one dozen countries, comes together to level up their winter skills. A mix of personalities, nationalities, and egos bring out the best—and the worst—as these globally elite men and women work and play together. They rub elbows with hardy locals and a group of scientists gathered close by …

One fatality is almost expected with this training. A second is tough but not a surprise. However, when a third goes missing? It's hard to not be suspicious. When the missing man is connected to one of the elite Maverick team members and is a special friend of Lieutenant Commander Mason Callister? All hell breaks loose …

Mountain hit the Arctic, knowing full well they would have to drag his dead body back out of the tundra before he ever quit on his little brother, Teegan. Theirs hadn't been the easiest of upbringings, but, when times had been tough, there'd always been the two of them.

Yet the series of events so far has gone from mysterious to downright deadly, and just what is the elusive Dr. Amelia's part in all this anyway? Like a ghost, she slips in and around everyone. What is her problem with the base, and, more important, what is her end game?

Dr. Amelia Morrison had seen too much in her life to trust anything she can't fathom with her own eyes. So, what she sees here makes no sense. Something is rotten at the Arctic international military training camp. She needs to stay close, but, deep inside, she just wants to run for cover. But this mountain of a man keeps her coming back, and his younger brother she manages to keep alive. However, saving a man out in these harsh elements is a completely different story than saving him from his fellow man.

Together, Mountain and Amelia need to solve this nightmare, before no one else is left alive …

Sign up to be notified of all Dale's releases here!

https://geni.us/DaleNews

PROLOGUE

PUZZLED, MOUNTAIN STARED at Chef Elijah. "None of us can figure out why. Why would you do such a thing?" he asked the big, likable man.

Chef shrugged, didn't say anything, and crossed his arms over his chest. He remained silent.

"See? It doesn't make sense. There's no motive. There's absolutely nothing. I don't have a clue why you would even try to knock out Teegan."

"Not saying nothing," Elijah replied through gritted teeth.

Then the door opened, and the colonel stepped in. Mountain stood and tilted his head. "Sir."

"Did you get any answers from him?"

"No, not yet," he replied in frustration.

The CO looked over at Elijah, disappointment evident in his expression. "I don't know what the hell you've been playing at or how long you've been at it," he muttered, "but you've sure as hell disappointed a lot of people."

Elijah closed his eyes and didn't say anything. Mountain watched the two of them, sensing a way-bigger betrayal happening here, as Chef and the CO had been friends for a very long time.

"I'm sorry, sir. He doesn't want to talk, and I've been at it for a couple hours now," Mountain confirmed, as he stretched his large frame.

"Oh, I can talk to him," the colonel declared. "Might be the best thing for both of us. We go way back."

"Not alone, sir," Mountain noted, a warning in his tone.

The CO nodded. "No, of course not." He glared at Elijah. "A damn nuisance this is," he muttered. "And here I was looking forward to my breakfast."

"We can't let him back into the kitchen, not after …"

The colonel shot a hard look at their beloved and trusted chef and then left the room.

Mountain shook his head at Chef. "I don't know what the hell's going on here," he admitted in a low voice, "but I don't believe it for one second."

"Mountain!" The shout came from the other side of the door. As he stepped out to the hallway, leaving a guard on Elijah, Magnus raced toward him. "What's up?" Mountain asked, with a fierce gaze.

"You've got a visitor," he said, "and unfortunately she's hurt."

His eyebrows shot up. "She? Who is it?"

"It's Amelia," Magnus confirmed, as excitement filled his voice—panic too. "She got here on her own, but she's hurt, and she's hurt bad. I've got her in with Sydney, but you need to come—now."

DAY 1

MOUNTAIN BEAR RODE raced to the clinic, his footsteps thundering in the hallway, dodging people who turned to stare. Already a crazy buzz filled the air, and that was before anybody on base had heard about Amelia's arrival. Knowing that Chef Elijah was being interrogated and was banned from the kitchen was enough to set the entire place on edge. The rumors were rampant, and everyone was divided on the subject. Mountain couldn't imagine what was going through their minds at this point. Hell, he was in the same boat himself and couldn't clarify the thoughts in his own head.

It felt so wrong to think that Elijah was involved in any way with any of the madness that had plagued this base and this particular survival session, especially any intentionally drugging of Teegan, Mountain's brother. One theory was that both brothers had been drugged, via their dinner plates set aside for them that night. However, there must have been a bigger dose for Mountain, but Teegan got it instead, explaining his dangerous reaction thereafter.

Now it seemed more nefarious.

This drugging of Teegan could not be passed off as somebody else's dirty deed. With everybody eating Chef's food over these last twelve weeks and counting, a lot of questions arose regarding the recent illnesses that had spread through the place—not to mention whispers of poison. Mountain couldn't imagine that their beloved Chef would have done that. Yet somebody had obviously done something, and they needed answers fast.

But *fast* didn't mean accepting answers that weren't correct. Mountain and both investigation teams, covert and overt, must have the facts in order to truly get to the bottom of all this. He couldn't imagine how the CO felt right now either. That had to be one of the worst things to deal with, considering the longstanding close relationship between the colonel and Chef. Mountain himself had dealt with enough in-house betrayals to know how rough that was.

When he reached the clinic, the door was closed. He gave a perfunctory knock and stuck his head inside, grateful it wasn't locked. Sydney looked over at him and glared, but he stepped inside and closed the door behind him. "How is she?" He tried to keep his voice low but failed, as it came out more as a harsh roar.

Sydney winced, then told him to keep his voice down and returned to her patient.

Mountain saw the blood dripping from the hospital bed to the floor. He stared at Sydney and asked again, "Oh my God, how is she?" Again his attempt to keep his voice calm and quiet went out the window, as the question came off as a heavy growl.

Sydney glared at him. "Stop interrupting me," she stated in a tone that matched his mood.

With that, he had to shut up, as Sydney worked feverishly on the poor woman. Mountain walked closer and pulled the blanket out of the way and saw a fresh bullet wound oozing, the source of all the blood.

He sucked in his breath, glaring down at the evidence in

front of him. Shaking his head, he muttered, "Good Christ, she was shot? What the hell?"

"Yeah, that would be my take, and this isn't the only one." She indicated the second bullet wound, and he looked at her in shock.

"Did she say anything?" he asked, speaking urgently.

"Yes, that she tried hard to not come here, but I was her only chance of survival now."

He stared down at Amelia. "Why didn't she come in before? Did she say anything at all that would tell us why?"

"I don't know if it means anything, after her first few words. She was in shock, and, by the looks of it, she's got old wounds that she's dealing with as well. I haven't had a chance to get to those yet because I'm too busy trying to stop the bleeding in the two fresh wounds," she shared, cleaning out one now.

As more blood welled up, she started cursing, and he winced. Sydney was overwhelmed, and, no matter how good of a doctor she was, she didn't have all the resources she needed.

"Put me to use," he declared.

"I need a nurse in here to help," she replied, still working feverishly.

"No time for that, and I've got an awful lot of field dressing experience." She gave him a sharp look, and he gave her a flat one back. "Come on. Tell me what you need."

And, with that, she barked orders that he struggled to keep up with, but, about twenty minutes later, she gave him a nod, as if acknowledging his help. "We might have beaten it." She watched anxiously, as she released the tourniquet slowly, waiting to see if the blood would start pouring again, but instead it appeared to ease back.

She sucked in her breath in relief. "A slight reprieve." She quickly pulled back the covers and checked the rest of Amelia's body, looking for more wounds. He waited, his gaze equally discerning, as they both sorted through the wounds. When he saw torn flesh and the puckering of a closing wound high up on her shoulder, he sucked in his breath. "That's another bullet hole."

"It is," she agreed, "but it's also weeks old."

"Jesus," he muttered, the shocks continuing to reverberate through his system, as he realized that not only had Amelia been shot but she'd been recently shot at two different times. The first time had been earlier, and she had done amazingly well at tending to herself, cleaning and stitching up her wound. Still, the second shooting had dropped Amelia to the point that she needed someone else to give her a hand. He wondered what it would have taken for her to come here for aid, and now he knew.

"The only reason she wouldn't have come," Sydney guessed, looking at her patient intently, "is that Amelia had to be suspicious of the person who shot her the first time and the possibility that it's someone from here."

"That's a huge leap," Mountain noted.

She glared at him. "I'm in the business of huge leaps."

He winced at that because, in some ways, so was he. Sometimes those leaps were all he had in order to make the next set of questions rise to the surface to be answered, and those answers often took him right back around the same circle.

"I can't imagine what she went through," he murmured, with a tic in his jaw revealing how close he was to losing control of his temper. "She was out sledding, which is exhausting, especially with that shoulder still healing from an earlier bullet wound."

"These two more recent wounds are worse. However, one appears to be much more superficial. The other one she took through her side. I can't find any damage on the inside," she shared, and he looked at her skeptically. "Yeah, I've already checked. I don't want to stitch her up though, not until the bleeding has fully stopped." Sydney sagged back a step, looked down at her bloody hands and the pools of blood on the floor. "That poor woman."

Mountain checked the bruises on Amelia's shoulders and her legs. Her body was heavily and quite decently muscled, yet looked to have suffered for the last while. She was lean—almost too lean. "Is there anything else she needs from us right now?" he asked.

"She needs blood, but that's not happening here. She's cold, and we need to get her covered back up soon," Sydney replied, checking Amelia's vitals. "I staunched the bleeding, so now I can stitch her up. Then we'll bandage her and get her as warmed up as we can. I can do the bandage part, so you go see if you can roust up something warm for her."

"Heated blankets?"

"Sure, although, with Elijah out of commission and not in the kitchen, you'll have to check in with Avalon and Chrissy."

"I'll sort it out." Mountain walked to the sink, quickly washed his hands, and then headed to the kitchen. As he got there, he found the two women busily working.

Avalon winced at him. "Don't know where you've been," she admitted, squinting her eyes and checking him over, but then her face relaxed. "You're still standing, so I presume you won."

He glanced down and noted he hadn't gotten all the

blood washed off his arms. He nodded. "I need a heated blanket, so if you have any way to make that happen, let's do it as quickly as you can, please."

"Yeah." She pointed to the heaters on the side. "We have blankets set aside just for Sydney." She didn't say anything more, just quickly popped a blanket in one machine and pushed the button.

In a few minutes, Mountain stepped out of the kitchen, a warm blanket tucked up close, and he raced back to the medical clinic. As he got in there, Sydney was putting the final bandage on.

"Bandages are a good sign," he said, as he carefully covered their patient with the still-warm blanket.

"Yeah, she's holding her own at the moment, and I'll keep her knocked out for now, so she doesn't destroy my handiwork by moving too much." He frowned at that, but Sydney shook her head. "I understand how you feel. It would be nice if we didn't have to do that, but I can't have her opening any of the stitches. She'll hemorrhage, and we'll lose her," she stated flatly.

That was a stark reality. When it came to medical experience, Sydney had the final say.

"Fine, but I need to know if she says anything."

"If she says anything right now, it won't be coherent, and you can't go with it."

"I don't care if it's coherent or not," he argued. "We need answers, and she's got the bulk of them."

"Maybe so," Sydney admitted, "but Amelia's also the most injured witness you have had so far and will be largely incoherent for quite a while. So I'll keep her drugged for now, at least until I'm satisfied that I can get her out of this without any problems. I need her airlifted out pronto, but the weather out there is shit."

He nodded. "I guess in that case, I'm staying here then."

"Why?"

He shrugged. "I won't take a chance of her saying something and me missing it, not to mention a repeat performance to harm her. Remember what happened to Carl."

"Fine," she agreed. "As long as I don't need that other bed, you can have it." She pointed to the second hospital bed off to the side.

He gave her a small smile. "How many times has this bed been used as surveillance during this training session?"

"Too many," she replied, "as in, seriously too many times. Honest to God, I've lost count."

He gave a half laugh. "The good news is that, with her arrival and with your magical hands," he noted, with a smile in her direction, "Amelia should pull through."

"I really hope so," Sydney said. "You need to inform the colonel, and we should get word out to her family." Mountain frowned at that, and she watched the expression on his face change. "Obviously you don't agree with that idea, and you need to tell me why."

"Somebody tried to kill her, not once but twice—that we know of. Since I have no idea who that might have been, I would just as soon keep it quiet for now. Plus, nobody seems to think she's missing," he pointed out. "As a matter of fact, they all seem to think that she's very capable out there."

"I agree," Sydney replied. "And I think, in this case, if it weren't for human interference, she *is* very capable, but, the fact of the matter is, somebody shot her."

"Exactly. So, I would prefer to keep her presence here as

secret as possible, for as long as we can, at least until she can get back on her feet anyway."

She gave him a sideways look. "Her family?"

He frowned. "I may have to go to the village."

"How can you go to the village and keep an eye on her?" she pointed out, with a bright smile.

He shook his head. "At the moment I have no clue. First things first. I'll stay close and confirm that she makes it through the night."

"Then we'll both be here," she declared, with a warning glance at him, "because I have no intention of leaving her, not until she's a bit more stable." And that was the last she had to say on it.

He pulled up a chair and texted Magnus. When a knock came on the door a few minutes later, Sydney looked over at him, and he shrugged. "That'll be Magnus."

She walked to the door and let Magnus in.

"Nobody else comes in or out," Mountain ordered.

"Not even a nurse?" Magnus asked.

"Nobody. Just Sydney, me, and now you."

Magnus studied him, then nodded and walked over for a closer look at the woman on the bed. "What do we know?"

Mountain let Sydney give Magnus a rundown of Amelia's physical ailments, his expressions mirroring Mountain's when he had heard about the recent double gunshot wounds. "Jesus," Magnus muttered. "No wonder she didn't want to come in. She was already injured and probably figured somebody here shot her—or maybe she knew it for sure."

Fuming, Mountain tried to conceal his emotions, but the tic in his jaw gave it away. He did keep his tone under control, as he added, "I wonder if she was hoping that, by now, whoever would look after her medical care would note the old wounds and the new, recognizing the need to keep her safe. For her, coming here had to be a giant leap in faith and trust."

"You can count on that," Sydney stated. "However, keeping her safe in this hellhole right now may be a whole different story."

"And yet you would think, with the latest development, we should be free and clear," Magnus noted, his gaze going from one to the other.

She shrugged. "I'm not convinced it was Elijah," she shared. "So, no, I certainly don't feel that sense of relief."

Magnus looked over at Mountain. "What about you?"

"Something's off here," he replied bluntly. "I don't know what, and, until I get answers, I'm not sure how this will play out. Elijah is a wild card, but I don't believe for a second that he could shoot someone. Plus, who shot at you and the sled dogs? I don't see Elijah doing that either. Has he confessed? No. Has he explained anything? No. The whole thing obviously has the colonel pretty upset, but I'm not certain of anything at this point in time."

"So, you don't believe this nightmare is over with?" Magnus asked.

"I'm sure it isn't. We don't have a motive yet either," Mountain said. "Until we get that, I'm not sure I can say either way."

Magnus eyed him carefully, then Sydney. "Are you guys not telling me something?"

"No. We don't know anything to *not* tell you yet," Mountain pointed out, and his words had that same flinty tone he took on when he needed to end an argument. "The bottom line is, I don't want to leave Amelia alone in case she says something tonight, awake or asleep. Although Sydney doesn't seem to think that Amelia will say anything that's worth noting. Still, I don't want to take the chance of missing something." He stared at Magnus. "I can't afford to."

Magnus nodded at that. "Makes sense to me, so I presume you're staying here on watch."

"I am, at least for now, which means you need to keep an eye on the rest of the base."

"If we keep our chef under guard, that should help. We're also trying to keep the news and everybody's interpretation of the news about Elijah's supposed involvement low-key, as long as that is worth doing."

"Which won't work," Sydney noted. "People here already know that he's been picked up and is being held by the investigative team in our makeshift jail, otherwise known as the storage room. The base doesn't know why, and they don't know what he's done, but, considering all the shit going on around this place, it could get ugly."

"Ugly how?" Mountain asked her. "What is it? Are you picking up something that we aren't?"

"Outside of the fact that everybody is upset, I haven't heard a whole lot," Sydney replied, taking a deep breath. "However, if you think about it, it won't take them long to realize what's happened, and, when they do, I suspect you'll have people reacting to Elijah in a pretty ugly way. It's not as if they haven't noticed his absence from the kitchen already. Avalon and Chrissy are handling the food, but Elijah has been the one constant in this place, since the very beginning."

"We've got a guard on him, just in case," Magnus shared.

"Sorry to burst your bubble, but I don't think one guard

is enough," she argued bluntly. He looked at her in surprise, and she shrugged. "Some pretty upset people are out there, not to mention the fact that we have thirty or so highly trained people from almost a dozen countries cooped up in this place."

"Right. I'll be on guard duty from time to time then, I guess," Magnus responded, as he turned back to Mountain.

Mountain studied him intently, then shook his head. "Set up three teams of three. I don't think one at a time will be enough."

"Got it. First let's see if we can make it through tonight." He looked down at the sleeping woman and asked no one in particular, "Will she wake up anytime soon?"

"No," Sydney declared, her tone flat. "I made sure of that. I can't take a chance of her injuring herself, fighting me off or fighting whatever nightmare she has when she wakes up. I just now got the bleeding under control, but any struggle from her will destroy all my handiwork. We can't risk it right now. She's lost an awful lot of blood. I can't do a transfusion here, so keeping her under, while her body works to recover, is the best I can do."

"Understood," Magnus said, as he looked back at Mountain. "While I'm here, do you want to take off and grab your laptop or anything else you might need? I presume you won't let me relieve you during the night."

"No, I won't, and you'll have plenty to do anyway, as you secure the base. And, yes, I'll go grab my laptop and a jacket and maybe pick up some coffee and food."

"I'm not sure about the food status," Magnus noted.

"Food's coming," Mountain said. "I went down there and grabbed a hot blanket a while ago, and the two women were hard at work on our meals." With that, he got up, walked over to stare at the sleeping woman and shook his head. "This behavior is the kind we would expect from one of us, if we were in enemy territory, anticipating a poor reception. It's not something we expect out of a neighboring scientist and certainly not somebody staying out in these Arctic conditions," he muttered, a deep crease between his eyebrows. "Getting shot was an obvious life-or-death issue," he noted. "Yet she managed to deal with the first gunshot incident quite efficiently, I would say. However, this most recent attack, the second attempt, that's the one that did her in. God damn it, I want to find the bastard who did that." He glared at Magnus. "Give me five minutes." And, with that, he quickly disappeared.

AMELIA SHIFTED, PAIN slammed into her, gasping, even more pain slammed right back.

"Take it easy," a woman said from her side in a gentle tone.

Amelia moaned, not able to orient herself. She started to panic.

The same woman spoke again. "I'm checking that the bleeding has stopped," she explained, "and then I'll give you something for the pain."

Sure enough, the pain eased again, as Amelia drifted in and out of consciousness. She slept several more times, only to wake to the same pain again, then to immediately crash back down. When she woke yet once more, she heard a different voice. A male—strong, deep, and dark. She couldn't place that voice either and felt herself fighting it, afraid. His words told her that she was safe and that she was getting the medical help she needed, but it didn't ease her fears.

She didn't remember needing medical help. She didn't remember anything, and that part bothered her. She shifted and once again cried out with pain. Warm hands reached out with a wet washcloth and gently wiped her face and her neck, before a woman whispered, "Go back to sleep." Amelia immediately dropped back under, happy to get away from a world so seemingly unpleasant. The additional whispered words came from a man. "You are safe now. I'll make sure of it." His words were so faint that she thought she had imagined them.

When she surfaced again, she had no idea of time or space; her world had completely changed. She didn't know where anything was or who anyone was. She raised her eyelids and stared straight ahead. The light was dim, and she was on something soft, like a bed, and sheets covered her. The blankets were warm too, so, wherever she was, she was obviously being cared for, and that was both good and bad. She didn't know why, but a feeling of doom underlaid all this comfort.

She stared around the room in confusion. The lights were low, so much so that she could see but not enough. Her mind was clear though, and, for that, she was grateful. When a quiet voice beside her spoke, she shifted and then gasped in pain. Immediately a hand reached out and squeezed hers, a hand that felt both familiar and foreign. She looked down at it, trying to concentrate and to recognize who this might be. When a huge male figure loomed large above her, she gasped and shrank back.

"It's all right," he said.

It was the same soothing voice she'd heard many times

throughout the night.

"My name is Mountain. I'm not here to hurt you," he explained. "I'm here to protect you."

She blinked at him several times. What kind of a name was that? Who was this person? And what the hell did she need protecting from? Nothing made any sense. She closed her eyes and willed it all away. Much later she heard the same voice call out to her.

"Easy now, just wake up. Take it easy. You're okay."

She shifted and winced in pain.

"Yeah, that side will hurt you," he confirmed, a compassionate note in his voice.

She turned her head to find him staring down at her. "Where am I?" She spoke in a whisper.

"You're in the military training base," he replied.

Her eyes widened in shock, even as she tried to process what that meant.

He added, "You're safe, and we're keeping an eye on you. You haven't been left alone for a moment."

She struggled with that too because none of it made any sense.

"And, in case you don't remember," he shared in that same calm, patient, and soothing tone, completely at odds with the size of the man in front of her, "you came here after being shot—for a second time, I might add—with two bullets hitting you most recently."

She blinked at him, not comprehending anything.

He nodded and repeated, "Just know that we're looking after you, and you're safe."

"Yet obviously I wasn't," she murmured.

"Obviously not," he agreed, with a nod. "I'm really hoping you can talk to me, although I know our good doc will shut me down the moment she finds out you're awake."

Amelia stared at him. "I'm not at all sure I'm very awake. I'm not sure I'm awake at all," she shared, as she shifted carefully, realizing that every movement was agonizing.

"I understand that too," he told her calmly. "Remember. You've been shot very recently in the side, and the older wound is up on your shoulder. So, no matter which way or how you move, it'll hurt."

"*Great*," she muttered, and then her eyes opened wide. "My dogs."

He looked at her in surprise. "Did you bring them here?"

She blinked several times and then whispered, in a near panic, "I don't remember."

"I'll check," he said, standing up now. "Don't you worry. If your dogs are here, we'll find them. We've got somebody here to look after the sled dogs."

"Joe," she whispered immediately.

He frowned at her intently. "Do you know Joe?"

She gave somewhat of a nod. "I think he has them."

"I'll check," Mountain repeated. "Now don't you worry. Just relax and go back to sleep." He sat back down, and she even heard the clicks on his phone, as he texted someone.

"Tell me if he has them," she demanded, but her eyelids were still closed, knowing that any movement would hurt. Still, she couldn't rest until she knew.

When his phone buzzed, he sighed in relief, and then told her in a pleasant tone, "Joe has them. They're doing fine, chilling with his pack."

She gave him a twisted smile. "Good."

With that, she immediately fell back asleep again.

DAY 2 MORNING

AMELIA WOKE WITH a start, her eyes wide. She stared around, not moving her head, aware that she was finally back to the land of the living, and yet she couldn't recall everything that had led up to her arrival in this place. She hoped for more answers, and, as she rolled her head to the side, it landed on the electric gaze of the huge man sitting beside her. She blinked again, thinking she might have imagined him, but he was still here.

He got up, walked over, and asked gently, "How are you feeling now?"

"Water?" she asked in a raspy voice.

He immediately held out a glass for her, and she drank deeply. When she had emptied the glass, he asked, "Do you want more?"

"No, I'm good." She sagged back and took a moment to recover from the pain of her exertions, closing her eyes.

"My name is Mountain," he offered, and her lips twitched at that.

She opened her eyes and gave him an odd smile. "Did your parents have any idea what size you would be?"

"No, I don't think so," he replied, with a laugh. "Apparently they guessed, and I would say correctly."

She gave him a small smile. "You've been here looking after me, haven't you?"

"I have been," he confirmed. "Though *looking after you* might be an exaggeration of my skills, but I've definitely been keeping an eye on you. We do have a doctor for the true *looking after.*"

She looked over at him. "Do you know what happened?"

"No, and I'm really hoping that you can tell me."

She frowned, as she stared up at the ceiling again. "It's pretty hazy," she muttered and glanced at him. "You also look familiar."

"That could be for a lot of reasons," he explained calmly. "I think I saw you in the village once or twice, although mostly in passing. I don't think we ever spoke. You may also have been to this base and seen me because I've certainly been here plenty of times. However, I don't know that we've ever been introduced."

She swallowed and winced at the pain reverberating up her side. "Where's the doc?" she asked, her pain evident in her tone and her breathing.

"She'll be back in a minute," he replied, checking the time. "She stepped out to grab some coffee for us," he shared, with a note of amusement. "She'll be back soon."

She heard his words and then it hit. "Coffee?" Suddenly a hint of hope filled her tone.

He snorted. "I'm glad to see you're on the mend, but I'm not sure that the doc will let you have coffee this soon." She gave him a frown, but he wasn't swayed either way. "An awful lot of people need to hear what happened to you, so anything that would get your brain kicked in and functioning would help."

"In that case, I need coffee," she stated firmly.

The door opened then, and Amelia watched, without moving too much, as a graceful woman of about her age stepped into the room, carrying coffee for two. Another man was at her side, and both of them were laughing. As they approached, Sydney looked over in delight. "Wow. Look who's awake."

Amelia gave her a slight smile. "Apparently I owe you my life."

Sydney shrugged. "I don't know about that," she argued, with the same enthusiasm. "I certainly would have preferred to see you *before* you got into this shape, particularly since you didn't come to me after you'd been shot the first time."

Amelia gave her a flat stare, then looked at what was in her hand. "Mountain said there's coffee."

"Did he offer you coffee?" Sydney asked curiously.

"No, he explained I probably wouldn't be allowed to have any."

Sydney chuckled. "And I suppose you disagree." She came over, picked up a blood pressure cuff, and immediately checked Amelia's vitals. When Sydney was finished, she noted the data on her e-tablet, ignoring everyone else around her.

When she stopped tapping on the screen, Amelia broke the silence in the room. "So, what's the verdict on the coffee?"

Looking at her carefully, Sydney spoke. "You're more concerned about the coffee than anything else?"

"If anybody starts asking me questions, believe me, I will need coffee."

"We can send Magnus down to get you a cup," she offered, turning to look at Magnus, as he nodded with a smile. "Do you take it black?"

"I'll take it any way I can get it," Amelia replied, "particularly right now."

With a chuckle, Magnus nodded and quickly walked out of the clinic, taking Mountain with him.

Sydney looked down at her patient. "Now, while the men are gone, I want to check your wounds, if that's okay with you."

"Are you afraid the coffee will leak out?" Amelia asked, with interest.

Sydney burst out laughing. "Oh, a sense of humor. I like that."

"Sometimes it's all we have," Amelia shared.

Sydney stopped to focus on her and nodded. "Sounds as if you and Mountain have been having quite the conversation."

Amelia slowly lowered her lashes, as she considered that. "He's looking to find out what happened, but so am I."

"You don't remember?" Sydney asked lightly, as she continued to check over Amelia.

"Let's just say, things are a bit on the fuzzy side."

"Let's start with some basics, which I need you to understand," the doc began. "You've been shot, and I'm talking about the fresh wound on your side. You've lost an awful lot of blood, and I don't have any here," she pointed out. "So, you are not to move. You're not to do anything that would stress the stitches or would cause any bleeding. If I had to go back in to try to stop the bleeding, that in itself could kill you."

Amelia stared at her. "Of course," she whispered. "I hadn't considered that."

"No, and yet, even now, you're wondering how to get out of here," the doc stated, looking at Amelia closely. "You need to stop thinking about that. You can't even think about that because, if you open any of those wounds," she repeated,

"I can't save you. Your blood count is critically low. The only remedy for that is to get your blood built back up again, and that'll take some time. You're weak, and you won't get out of this bed anytime soon. A simple fall now could start the bleeding again and could literally kill you. I'm not sure how you made it here, but I'm grateful that you came, so that we could at least try to do our best for you."

Amelia wasn't sure what to say to that. The woman appeared to be sincere, but she was from here, this godforsaken military base.

Sydney hesitated and then added, "We're doing our best to keep you safe. There has to be a reason why you didn't come in for help, back when you took that first bullet," she noted, taking a moment to stress her point, "and that's disturbing. Yet the fact that you did come in when you realized the second wound was more than you could handle is a good thing. If you had waited any longer, you wouldn't have made it."

Amelia winced. "That's why I came when I did," she admitted, "but it was with the fatalistic knowledge that I could be signing my own death warrant."

"I'm so sorry for that," she replied. "I know Mountain will keep you under guard because we aren't sure what's happened or who shot you. That is unacceptable on any side, but we also know that you have friends, family, and connections with the locals, so we also must consider whether anybody there may have had something to do with this."

Amelia looked at her in surprise. "You guys don't know who shot me?"

"No, we don't," the doc confirmed. "We've all been hoping that you could tell us."

"No, I can't," Amelia replied, "and that's bad news then,

for all of us."

MOUNTAIN STEPPED INSIDE the medical clinic. He'd been listening on the opposite side of the door, staying in the background, letting Sydney do her doctoring thing. He stepped forward just then and smiled down at Amelia. "Anything that you can remember will be a help," he said in a casual tone. "I need to sort out who shot you, but I also need to sort out a bunch of other issues that have been going on here in our base."

She looked at him and stated waspishly, "Your base is a mess."

He winced at her blunt tone but nodded. "You're right. It has been, but some of that came from your scientists' camp too."

She frowned.

Mountain studied her intently, wondering for a moment if she was aware of the issues pertaining to the untimely demise of her colleagues. "I don't know if you've heard all of what happened." Then he quickly filled her in on Anna and Myles.

Amelia's eyes widened, as she stared at him in shock.

He nodded. "So, as much as I can see that, from your perspective, we're to blame for all this," he explained in a teasing tone, "from where I sit, with a little bit of care and understanding, an awful lot is going on here that I don't think you've known about."

"Good Lord," she whispered.

He picked up her hand, lacing her fingers with his.

She went quiet and stared at their hands. "I feel as if you

did this before."

"During the night," he shared, "as you had a lot of nightmares and kept tossing and turning. I needed to keep you calm, so you wouldn't rip everything open and start bleeding again. Sydney would have had my head if anything happened to you," he shared, with half a smile. "She spent the better part of the day stitching you up and ensuring all the bleeding was taken care of."

She stared at him, and he was struck by a very odd look on her face. He shrugged. "I certainly wouldn't do anything to hurt you while you were sleeping. We're all very concerned about your survival. We need you to survive," he added in quick succession, and she was taken by surprise.

"Why is that?" she asked in a curious tone. "If you know that I was shot before and that I didn't come in, then I must not trust anybody here, including you."

As he studied her, his gaze was hard, but then he nodded. "You are entitled to feel that way," he admitted, with an intensity in his blue eyes. "Obviously you're on the outside looking in, so you don't know who here is working in the shadows and who can and cannot be trusted," he argued in a calm tone. He really needed her to trust his people, and that was crucial in getting her help. "I won't ask you to trust everyone here, and that's why you're under guard, but you do need to trust Sydney. She's your doctor, and she's gone to great lengths to keep you alive. I've been here since you were first brought in."

"I can't imagine why." Her tone was curt.

He understood the sentiment. "Partly to see if you can tell us anything about what happened to you."

She snorted, then laughed in a mocking tone.

"And partly to keep you safe because you were already

shot twice, and I can't afford to have a third shot take you out this time."

That caught her attention, and she looked at him with a searching gaze, as if trying to understand what really made him tick.

"Whoever has been shooting you, or shooting at you, is undoubtedly still determined, and I don't want him to succeed," he declared bluntly. He couldn't read the odd look in her gaze, but she'd had a lot to assimilate in a very short time.

When Sydney stepped back in to join them, he looked over at her. "Will Amelia be okay?"

Sydney gave him an unreadable look, which meant *maybe*, or at least that's as far as he was prepared to interpret it. She gave a half shrug. "Obviously she's in a pretty dicey situation, and we need to ensure that her bleeding doesn't start up again. If that happens, it's as good as a death sentence. However, as far as I can tell at the moment, if we can keep her calm and not moving, then we have a good chance of getting her through this."

He looked back down at their patient, whose gaze went back and forth from one to the other. "She came with her dogs, and she left them with Joe," Mountain shared.

Sydney stared at him in surprise. "Seriously?"

Mountain nodded. "She was concerned enough to ensure that the dogs were taken care of before she came in."

Sydney looked down at her patient, and, by the looks of it, she was impressed with how Amelia had handled herself so far. "That was kind of you," Sydney noted, "and I appreciate that you were looking after the dogs, but you also need to look after yourself."

Amelia sighed. "I came in here," she pointed out in a

disgruntled tone. "The rest is up to you."

"Remember that you don't always get what you want, and, when I insist on bed rest and keeping you medicated for pain and movement," Sydney pointed out, "it is for your own good."

"I understand."

"You have a catheter also, and you don't need to move anywhere," Sydney added. "So no complaints. I really can't afford to lose you out here." Such passion filled her tone that Mountain himself was hard-pressed not to reinforce her words, but it was obvious that Amelia wasn't protesting.

Amelia winced several times throughout the conversation, and, by the end of it, she studied Sydney, as if she were something new to her. "I could use something for the pain now," Amelia murmured, "though coffee would be lovely too."

Mountain snorted. "You can have coffee after the pain-killers."

Sydney quickly gave her some morphine to manage the pain level. "No coffee. Not for now. Expect to sleep for the rest of the day."

"I don't feel bad about that," she murmured. "Honestly I feel like shit."

"Take a timeout then," Sydney ordered. Amelia went under, as the morphine took hold of her. "This will be a long recovery," Sydney noted, as Amelia slipped into a deep sleep.

The doctor kept her patient mostly sedated over the next two days.

DAY 4 LATE AFTERNOON

W HEN AMELIA WOKE this time, she felt marginally better. *Marginally* was definitely the word that she would use in this instance because everything still hurt like crazy. She didn't even know what day it was or how much time had passed since she'd first shown up at this place. She had no idea what happened recently, outside of her pain, followed by more pain. Not to mention the nightmares here and there.

The fact that her dogs were being cared for meant that she could sink into her own healing. She desperately needed to regain her strength, so that her body could handle whatever was still to come. It was hard to relax, and the drugs were the only reason that she was as limp and as calm as she was. She understood perfectly well what would happen if any of the stitches broke loose and if the bleeding started up again. The doc was good, but she didn't have the resources up here to work miracles.

Amelia believed, for now, that, if anybody here would help her, it would be Sydney. Amelia had no reason to believe the doctor wouldn't. Meanwhile everybody kept reminding Amelia how she had been shot, and two different times, not that she wasn't already acutely aware of that. So somebody was out to ensure that she didn't survive. In her own head, she had narrowed it down and had concluded that the only place the shooter could have come from was here, on this military base. The shooter had to be from this base because the Inuit people had no motive to shoot at one of their own.

Now her problem was sorting out who had the opportunity to shoot her on both counts, assuming only one shooter, not two.

When the door to the clinic opened, and Mountain stepped in again, Amelia looked up in surprise.

He walked closer. "Hey," he said gently. "Glad to see you're awake."

She went to shrug and then held back. He had seen her reluctant movements, and she was amazed because nothing went unnoticed with this guy.

He nodded. "Just words, just use words."

"I'm awake and had not too bad of a night, but I think the pain woke me up."

"It'll be pain that wakes you up for quite a while," he shared, with a nod. "Even when you are healed on the surface, it takes time for flesh wounds to settle in. On the other hand, every time you wake up," he added, with a cheeky grin, "it's a win on a lot of levels."

His words were correct, but his tone was even more spot-on. It felt warm and compassionate; there was empathy, as if he understood exactly what she was going through.

"Let me help you get more comfortable," he offered, and, with her help, he carefully shifted her to a sitting up position and then walked back to Sydney's desk to retrieve a cup of coffee. "I brought it back for myself," he shared, "but I will cheerfully hand it off to you, if you think you can handle a little bit of it."

She looked at it with a longing. "I want it, but ..."

"Painkillers first?"

She winced. "It will be impossible to keep it down, without something to help."

He nodded. "Let me call Sydney." Then, instead of stepping out and away, he made a quick phone call, and Sydney arrived within seconds.

Amelia looked over at Sydney. "I hate to disturb you but …"

"I was already on my way over. Besides, that's what I'm here for." The doctor quickly did a full assessment and checked Amelia's vitals and then nodded, as if she were satisfied with her patient's progress. "Glad to see you're awake."

"I'm not sure if I am," she admitted, with a smirk. "I think the pain woke me."

"And it will for a while," she agreed, keeping a hand on her shoulder. "No other way it can't. That's the body's way of making sure that you get some help," she shared. "So, let's give you something to make it more comfortable."

"Appreciate it."

"Do you want a sip of coffee?"

"I would love it but …"

"Right. Let's give you the pain meds, and then we'll see where you're at afterward." And that's what they did. By the time the pain meds had done enough that she could breathe a little bit better, Mountain returned again, this time with a cup of coffee for her.

She looked at it and smiled brightly, under the mellowing effects of the meds. "I didn't think I would ever say no to coffee. However, I'm just not sure I can get it down."

Sydney immediately walked over and asked, "How's your throat?"

"Dry. It needs something. I just don't know what. I don't feel right."

"You won't feel right for a while," Sydney noted calmly. "Your body's been through a hell of an ordeal, and not for a little while, but for a long time. I would really love to know why the hell you didn't come in and get help the first time around."

She hesitated and then replied, "You may not know why I didn't come in. However, the question you really want to ask is, who am I afraid of?"

"Are you afraid of someone?"

"I can't answer that. I don't know," she admitted, "but I do believe that the shots came from somebody here. At least the camos were from here."

At that, Mountain stiffened. "So, you saw who shot you?" His words were slow, careful, as if confirming there was no misunderstanding.

"No, … I didn't see who shot me. I saw somebody soon afterward," she shared, "and he was moving at a good pace, but I don't know that he was the shooter. It's just, … I can't imagine so many people were outside at the time so that it wouldn't be him."

"Did he come upon you in a strange way? Did you get shot from a distance? Did it range from near or far? Do you know or have any idea of what happened?"

"This was the first shot. It was through and through," she clarified. "I was working, sitting with my dogs, up on the hillside, having a break. As I recall, … we were taking data readings." She thought back a bit, focused on some issue, and her eyes were scrunched up. "When the shot rang out, it hit me without any warning. I keeled over with the pain, and I was afraid. I thought maybe it had been an accident, only somebody came up on me almost immediately.”

“Did he say anything to you?”

She looked over at him with tears in her eyes and whispered, “*Good riddance*. I remember nothing else, and then he took off.”

“So, he left you out there to die?” he asked in surprise.

She nodded. “As far as I can figure, yes, me and my dogs.”

Mountain added, “I would think anybody who loves and appreciates these dogs wouldn’t have done that.”

“I agree,” she replied, “but it goes to show you just how wrong we can be. I guess that is the world we have come to create.”

Mountain sat back, obviously pissed off, if the motion of his jaw was anything to go by, but she kept swallowing her water. When she had enough, she looked at Mountain’s coffee and whispered, “May I have a sip?”

He immediately got up, walked over, and held it for her, so she could have a sip. “It’s not too hot at the moment, so you should be good.”

As it was, she had several sips, loving the feeling of the warmth, as it slipped down her throat.

When she returned the cup to him, she had managed to swallow about one-third of the coffee.

He smiled at her in a casual way. “Anytime you want more, you tell me.”

“Thank you,” she whispered.

“What else can you tell me about the guy who shot you? Did you see him? Anything you remember or any marker you may have seen?”

“He was in white winters,” she replied, stressing her words, “the kind when you don’t want to be seen. He blended in well."

"If dressed in white winters, that wasn't an accident at all," Sydney noted.

"No, not that I could tell. After he told me, *Good riddance*, I expected him to shoot the dogs. They were cut loose, but they stayed close."

"Sure they did. What happened then?"

"He left. I think he thought that I was a goner and that the dogs would take off, but my dogs, … they stayed close and kept me warm," she murmured. "After a bit I managed to get up and headed to the hideaway I had set up," she noted, and her voice trailed a bit, as if coming from afar.

Sydney got close to take her hand.

"I spent a few days inside, close with the dogs. I was trying to get them calmed down because they were pretty upset over the whole thing," she murmured. "Anyway, when I realized that I would live and that the bullet had missed anything vital, I started to get really angry, but I was also really wary. I didn't know the shooter or why he would want to kill me. So I stayed out of sight."

"How long ago was this?"

"I'm afraid I've lost track of time, being out there and now here. I feel as if it were quite a while ago," she replied.

Sydney nodded in agreement. "It's healed quite well, considering," Sydney admitted.

"It's healed, but I don't know about *quite well*," Amelia argued in a curt tone. "I stitched it but not easily, so it was what it was."

"Did you go to the village and ask them for help?"

"I got some herbs from one of the women," Amelia replied, with a careful tone. "They had a few remedies but not for bullet holes. They did have some medicines to help cut back the fevers, so all and all, I came out of that one pretty decently."

"So, when did you find Teegan?" Mountain asked.

AMELIA LOOKED UP at Mountain intently. "Teegan?" For the first time, she had fear in her eyes, as if hoping that he would not go any further down that line of questioning. Yet, of course, he would. Everybody here would, and he was one of them.

"Teegan is my brother," Mountain shared. "I came up north when he went missing."

Her gaze widened. "Good God," she muttered.

"So, did you find him? And keep him safe, until you couldn't do it anymore? Did you drop him off here? I've been searching for him every day."

At that, she stared at him. "Now I know who you are. I've … I have seen you."

"You've seen me all right, and gone to great lengths to avoid me," he stated, his gaze narrowing.

She gave him a flat stare. "That's nice. I guess that means you're on my do-not-trust list."

He snorted at that. "If I'm on your do-not-trust list, you're making a hell of a mistake, especially considering these last four days that you've been here, you were under my watch."

"Four days?" She blinked at him.

"Yeah, four days, mostly unconscious," he reiterated, "but, now that you're awake and seem to be doing fine, we do need answers." She let her eyes drift closed. "And, no," he stated, seeing her tactic to avoid him, "that won't get you out of it."

"Are you sure?" she asked, struggling to hold open her eyes. "If these were such major questions that you needed to ask," she argued, as her eyelids flickered shut again, "you should have done it before the painkillers took effect." And, with that, she closed her eyes and let herself drift back under.

Mountain sat here, waiting for her to wake up again. He wrote down notes, reasserting everything he knew so far about the whole mess.

Teegan had come to the clinic, as soon as he realized Amelia was awake, but, of course, she was back under again now. He stepped up beside his brother. "I know I feel like shit," he began, "but she looks like shit."

Mountain snorted. "She's still pretty feisty though."

He grinned. "It's what kept her going. You know that." Teegan patted his older brother on the shoulder. "Don't begrudge her the will to live, and even now … the will to keep herself safe."

"I won't," Mountain replied. He checked out his brother, and, as if he'd registered something, his gaze hardened. "Why aren't you in bed?" He glared at him.

"I'm healing and all that, and I'm doing a hell of a lot better. If I am not out as much as I can …" Mountain stared at him, warning Teegan with his gaze. Teegan shrugged. "Fine, fine. I was hoping to talk to Amelia and to at least thank her for saving my life," he admitted.

"And you'll get a chance, but not anytime soon. We can't have anything bothering her, upsetting her, or in any way making her move and disturbing her stitches," Mountain explained sternly. "She has to heal a little bit better first."

Teegan nodded. "She kept me alive." He stared down at

Amelia, a smile on his face. "And it takes somebody special to make the decision that she did to take me on out there in the wilderness and to heal me and to follow through on it." Teegan looked back at Mountain. "So she'll get my respect every time."

"She gets mine too," Mountain agreed, "and don't worry. I'm not begrudging her anything, but, if she knows something, no matter how small it is, we need that information."

Teegan nodded. "Did she say anything?"

"Yeah, she told me, when she was shot the first time, that the shooter came up to check on her after he shot her, saying, *Good riddance*, and cut the dogs loose, thinking they would take off on their own, I presume. Then he left her to die."

"Good God," Teegan murmured, staring at him in shock. "She thinks it's someone here? … It's one of us?"

"She told me that he was dressed in the all-white winter camo, which we all use whenever outside, so she's presuming it's us. I'm afraid that she's right too."

"Any idea who might have a beef with her?"

"She knows nobody in this base, as far as we know, although she took her dogs to Joe. She shouldn't have anybody who hates her here. I'll have to ask her, but I'm not willing to rule that out just yet."

"No, of course not," Teegan noted, "but still it sucks. She's done so much for me that it's hard to believe anybody could really want to hurt her."

"And yet somebody did want to hurt her," Mountain declared, "and in a big way. I have yet to ask her about the second attack because she went back under, due to the painkillers."

"So presumably, if that is all about the first attack, it's possible that the initial shooter found out she was still alive and went after her again—probably worried she could identify him, if only by his voice maybe."

"That's one of the assumptions we have to consider," Mountain said, with a nod. "But what happens now, when that person finds out she's still alive, which is my main concern."

Teegan looked at him intently. "Put me on the roster to guard her."

"No," Mountain declared, and he was not willing to give even one millimeter. "I'm not having you look after her, not when you're barely capable of looking after yourself."

"Hey, bro," Teegan barked, feeling hurt. "I know that, in your mind, you don't see me as being better or capable, but you're wrong. Plus, in this instance, you need additional help to protect her. I would do anything I can to keep her safe, so don't be foolish."

Mountain snorted, and that revealed all about where his mind was on the thought of Teegan helping.

Teegan continued with his argument. "I can help, even if it's sitting with her in the daytime, as backup for anyone, whatever," he offered in a frustrated tone. "She saved my life, so don't take away this opportunity for me to now help her." And, with that, he stepped to the door. "Let me know if she wakes up again. I'll go get some rest in the meantime." And, with that, he slowly headed out the door.

Sydney walked over to Mountain. "You need to cut Teegan a little bit of slack." He snorted, and she nodded at him sternly. "I understand. You've spent your lifetime looking after him, protecting him, being there for him, and, now that you've found Amelia, it's brought up this whole

Teegan went missing mess again. Nevertheless you need to ease up."

"She knows something," Mountain stated. "She knows a hell of a lot more than *something*, and, as soon as I mentioned Teegan, she deliberately floated back under again."

"You blame her?" Sydney asked, with a knowing smile. "She doesn't trust you, Mountain. She doesn't know you. She doesn't know anything about you. Yet here you are, demanding answers from her. Answers that she's probably not sure she should even give you," the doc suggested. "So cut her a bit of slack too." And, with that, Sydney walked back to her desk, sat down, and continued writing her notes.

He had no idea what she was doing but wouldn't argue with her. She was still the law when it came to the medical clinic, and this was her domain. As long as everybody here was functioning, doing well, and fit to do their duty on this base, he was prepared to leave the patients to her.

He looked down at Amelia and then back to Sydney. "Did you do a full body check on her?"

He had an odd tone to his voice, which Sydney picked up on immediately. "Yes, as did you."

He nodded. "I did, but I meant under her clothing and all. Does she have any tattoos? Anything identifiable I couldn't see? Does she have anything along that line?"

"No tattoos, at least nothing that came up on the initial check," Sydney clarified. "I didn't check her heels or soles. About her clothing"—she pointed off to the side—"you've already been through it once."

He nodded. "I'll go through it again." He hopped up and went over every piece very slowly. Amelia dressed in extremely high-quality clothing. However, at the end of the day, it was still just clothing. At least they were in good shape. They weren't brand-new by any means. Her boots were well broken in but had a good grip, good fit, and were rated for this type of cold. When he finally put down the last piece of her clothing, he sat once again and brooded.

Sydney walked over. "I know you want answers, but don't you go making yourself sick, so I have another patient." He looked over at her, struggling, and she nodded. "You can make yourself absolutely nuts over this," she pointed out, with a grin. "So why don't you give her some slack and let her recover a bit."

"We need answers before somebody takes her out again."

"I understand that. I get that, and we've got guards and all kinds of stuff happening," she noted. "I'm just telling you that you need to go a little bit easier on yourself." He glared at her, and she smiled. "Yeah, I also know that that glare is basically your go-to look when somebody says something you don't want to listen to."

"And you'll ignore it, I presume," he replied, with a note of humor.

"Absolutely." She laughed. "I've got a glare of my own for people who don't do what they're told," she declared, raising an eyebrow and glaring at him. "And, right now, you need to let Amelia rest a little bit longer. She's giving you more information every time she wakes up."

"She is," he agreed, with a nod. "Just not enough of it."

At that, she laughed. "Until you get to the bottom of all this, you won't be happy. Still, don't alienate everyone in the process."

"You do realize that only a few people have been out during these latest training sessions," he shared. "So I need to figure out who could possibly have shot her the second time."

"And I presume you've got someone doing a list, running down who it could be."

"Yeah," he muttered, with an odd exasperation. "The list is damn narrow, and Chef is on it." At that, she frowned and he nodded. "See? You don't like that answer any more than I do."

"No, I really don't, but, if that's where the answer is, then as long as you guys are certain …" She sent a look in his direction. "Then what am I supposed to do about it?"

"None of us can do anything about it, but, no, I'm not certain about Chef. Not yet anyway."

"Then maybe go talk to him, explain that Amelia has come in. I'll stay here with her anyway, so go do something useful for a change." When he stiffened and glared, she laughed. "I'm not scared of you, and I won't be intimidated by you." She added in a challenging tone, "So go on, go find something useful to do." And, with that, she pointed at the door.

He got up, with one last glance at the sleeping beauty on the bed. Then he faced Sydney. "You'll let me know if she wakes up, right?"

"I will," she stated. "So go, and, when you come back, maybe you'll have more answers and better questions."

And, with that, he turned and walked out.

DAY 5 MORNING

AMELIA WOKE UP, this time not feeling quite so rough, but her throat was sore, her eyelids heavy, and everything ached. As she shifted in bed, the doctor was immediately at her side. "Hey," Amelia greeted Sydney. "Did you sleep here?"

"I sleep right next door, and Mountain's been sleeping here every night to keep an eye on you," she shared, as she quickly checked over Amelia. "How are you feeling?"

"My throat's really sore," she whispered. "I'm not feeling all that bad. The pain's not terrible at the moment, but I'm not feeling good by any means."

"The *feeling good* part? … That'll take a while," Sydney shared. "Let's see if water helps with that throat." She moved away to get a glass and fill it. "Some of these drugs can make your throat feel quite dry."

Amelia had several large gulps and then nodded. "That feels a bit better."

"Good." Sydney eyed her closely. "You haven't had any food for a while. What do you think?"

"I don't know," she murmured. "I would love some food." She looked at the IV in her arm. "I guess that's how you've been keeping me alive, *huh*?"

"It is," Sydney confirmed, "but again our supplies are limited here. So the sooner I can get you off this, the better.

Getting you onto food is a good step, only I don't know how your stomach will handle it."

Amelia closed her eyelids. "Something soft. Maybe soup would be good."

"I'll send Mountain to the kitchen, as soon as I tell him that you're awake."

"Do you have to tell him that I'm awake?" There was a hard note to her voice.

"I do, and it doesn't matter, since he'll be here in a heartbeat anyway because he has that inner instinct that tells him when you're awake."

"I don't have all the answers he wants from me." Amelia rolled her head to the side, careful not to move her body much.

"You give him what you can give him and nothing more," Sydney stated. "If you don't know who you can trust and if you don't know anything about it, then you tell him that."

"He won't believe me," she said.

"He'll believe you because he won't have a choice. He won't like it, and it could definitely be something that you don't know that's helpful," Sydney added, "but I think that's really important for you to understand too. The fact that you already told him what you did helps a lot."

Looking bewildered, she frowned. "How does it help anything? I don't have a name. I don't even have a face."

"Did you see him?"

"Sure, but only with all his heavy gear on."

"Right." Sydney nodded, with a quick glance around. "And that's not quite the same thing, is it?"

"No, it isn't, since I couldn't identify him."

"Don't be so sure," she corrected. "What if you heard his

voice again? Are you sure that's not emblazoned into your mind?"

At that, she stared at Sydney, hearing the same snap of the voice. as it echoed in her mind. *Good riddance.* "Now that I might recognize," she admitted slowly. "But you've got to realize that it was outside, in the cold, and I was in this pain-altered state."

Sydney smiled. "Believe me, I do realize that, and so does Mountain. They're not trying to push or to hurt you. It's more a case of trying to get whatever information they can to keep you safe here. They're trying to figure out why somebody would have shot you in the first place. That is hard evidence that we can see. The question is, why were you shot?"

Amelia didn't know what to say to that, and then she remembered. "I might have seen something," she whispered.

"Hang on a minute." Sydney walked closer to her patient. "What do you mean, you might have seen something?"

"It was earlier that day," she began. "It was hazy out, and I wasn't even sure what I saw because of the white glare, but it's the only thing that I can think of."

"So, what did you see?"

"Several men were out that day, a long time ago, before I got shot the first time," she began, "and I saw two men separate and have a big argument, but I was quite a long distance away. I couldn't hear what the argument was. I couldn't see anything really. A storm was blowing. But, when I saw them again, … there was only one man. I only saw one man come back."

"You didn't see what happened to the other man?"

"No," she whispered. "I know I didn't see him again."

"When you say, you didn't see him again, how long ago

was this?"

"Weeks, weeks, and weeks," she replied, with an expression of deep thought.

Then the clinic door opened, and Mountain walked in.

Sydney immediately called him over. "She's wondering if all this is because of something she saw."

Mountain's eyebrows shot up, and his gaze turned to Amelia. He walked over and leaned close to her. "How are you feeling?"

"Like shit," she said, with half a smile, "but I do know that you weren't the one I saw."

"That's good news," he replied, with a light chuckle, hearing the loopy tone to Amelia's voice, due to the pain meds and all. "So, maybe if you let me off the hook and trust me a little bit," he told her, "we can get to the bottom of this. Now, tell me what you saw."

She explained about the storm, seeing two men in a verbal fight. "I don't even know that anything happened," she clarified. "There was a blur to it, and that's all I saw."

"And, when you saw the one man return alone, can you tell me anything about him?"

She shrugged. "Not really, it was too far to have a good look. I could tell he was big but not huge." She glanced at him. "Not your size."

"Nobody here is my size anyway," he replied, with a smirk and a half nod to the guy coming through the doorway. "Magnus is big, but he's not that big."

She nodded. "I don't even think he was his size, but I could be wrong." She frowned at the man who joined them. "Anyway, when I saw him again, it stuck out because I only saw one of them."

"So, the real question is, did he see you? Would they

have seen you in any way?" Mountain asked, looking at her. "When two were there or even after one returned, could you be seen? You need to think about this one carefully. You saw something, but did they see you?"

She shut her eyelids, as she thought back to that fateful day, a day that she had gone over many, many times, trying to figure out if that had anything to do with the situation she was in. "I don't know," she finally said, "but I was out there, so I guess it's possible."

"It's also a very good reason behind all this," Mountain stated, with a nod.

"If you say so," she muttered. "Personally, in my world, … I don't shoot people who might have seen me have an argument with somebody."

"What if it's an argument with somebody who didn't come back?"

"What do you mean?" she asked.

"What if it's an argument with somebody, and that somebody died or was killed because of this argument?"

She stared at him. "Meaning that he killed the guy he was having a fight with?"

"It's possible, or maybe he left him out there to die," Mountain suggested, "which, in these conditions, would be exactly the same thing."

She stared at him and shook her head. "I don't know. … Anything is possible. I just don't know. I didn't see the one again. I didn't think much of it, but I did think about it from time to time."

"What about the other one, the one still remaining?" Mountain asked, immediately picking up on her wording.

"I think I saw him another time, but I don't know for sure. You've got to remember. I'm out there miles away. I don't really have any way to ascertain one of you from another, not in your winter gear," she noted in an exasperated tone. "Sometimes whole groups of you are out there. Sometimes you split up during your war games," she pointed out, with a toss of her hand. "It's hard for anybody to tell you apart. I don't know," she cried out in frustration.

Mountain immediately grasped her hand. "And that's fine. You're not allowed to get upset now. So just relax."

She glared at him. "Gee, thanks for that," she muttered. "You might be a little too late."

He gave a boisterous laugh. "In a way, what you've said makes the most sense, but we need to talk about Teegan."

She stared at him. "One of the men I helped."

"Yes, those men. Why did you not bring them in?"

"Because the one man told me that they were shot by somebody on the base here," she shared, and then she frowned. "I'm not sure he said *shot*, but he definitely told me that we couldn't trust anybody on the military base."

"Okay."

"So, at that point, I didn't know what to do with them."

"You didn't take them to the village?"

"I did, to the one woman anyway," she replied, "the healer. She gave me a bunch of medicine and told me that I couldn't keep them there. They didn't want anything bad to happen to one of your guys in their settlement. It would not be good for them. Understanding that, I quickly took them back to one of my hideaways." At his raised eyebrows, she shrugged. "I've been up here annually for years."

"So, you have lots of these places here?"

"Yes, pretty much. I keep these little ice caves on my GPS. I have a few hideaways out there, where I can go without people finding me easily." She turned and looked at him. "And yet I do find that various people can be helpful."

"Are you the one who shot near us to show us the location of one ice cave out in the middle of nowhere?"

She looked at him and blinked. "I'm not sure." She frowned. "I don't think so. Do you want to tell me more about it?"

He shook his head at that. "It was just a question." He looked over at Magnus, whose narrowed gaze stared back at him.

"That was you and Teegan, wasn't it?" Magnus asked.

Mountain nodded. "Yeah, we were looking for Eric's hideaway. We found it, but the only reason we found it was because somebody in the distance was shooting at us."

"And you think that maybe they weren't shooting at you but around you? … To show you that location?"

"Right, but now I'm wondering if it wasn't to shoot us, and they accidentally shot up the location instead." He frowned, as he sat back and turned toward Amelia. "Can you tell us anything else about this same person who shot you later a second time?"

"No, not at all," she admitted, "and again I'm not even certain that he was the one who shot me both times. I just know that, when I was out there, this person looked similar. People have a way of moving that can be distinctive," she explained, "but I can't be sure because, when you're out in a training scenario such as this, if you have ten guys in a row, you might pick out one, but, when you see all ten separately, it's quite a bit harder."

"That is quite right."

"And it's not as if I get to sit there with binoculars and stare."

Mountain nodded. "That's fine, and we appreciate your

telling us."

She frowned at him, a wry look on her face. "Oh, I definitely get the impression that you would prefer if I had something else to say."

"Sure, I want very much for you to say that you know exactly who did this and point him out to me," he admitted, with a hard smile. "But I don't live in a fanciful world, and people have gone to great lengths to try and shut you up. Therefore, I need to confirm that whatever you do know, we know too, even if you don't think it's important. So, every time I see you, I'll ask you if you remember anything else, anything else you can identify." He gave her a smirk. "I won't stop until we get to the bottom of it."

She sagged against the bed and whispered, "Good luck then, because I've been trying to figure it out since all this started."

"Why did you send Teegan back when you did?" he asked suddenly.

She looked at him in surprise. "Because I'd just been shot, *again*, and it was all I could do to look after me," she replied. "I knew that he had come to the point where I thought maybe he would survive such a move, and I needed to take the chance because I was in bad shape myself."

"So, hang on a minute. You were shot, yet you put him on a sled, and you brought him to our military base. You left Teegan on the sled outside, where Elijah could find him, or you somehow informed Elijah that Teegan was out there. Then you took off, even though you were injured?"

She looked at him and then nodded. "Yeah, that sounds about right."

"Jesus," he muttered in an astonished voice. "Teegan is fine, by the way. You did save his life, and he's been busting down the doors trying to get at you ever since."

She smiled. "He's a nice man."

"He is a nice man," Mountain stated, "and, as I told you earlier, though I'm not sure you remember, he's my brother, and I care about him a great deal."

She smiled. "In that case, you need to be nice to me, if for no other reason than because I saved your brother."

"What we don't know is, how did my brother get into trouble in the first place."

She stared at him. "Oh."

"I guess you don't know either then, do you?"

"I don't know. I came upon him and the other one, at two different times, both of them injured, unconscious, and freezing in one of the little hollows that you guys make," she said. "I was trying to raise the alarm to get help. However, Teegan told me that it wasn't safe to let anybody know, that it was somebody from the military base." Then she frowned. "Or maybe the other man told me that." She shook her head. "I don't know. As it turned out, I couldn't do anything for him," she whispered, her voice sorrowful. "I really tried all I could, and, in the end, I delivered him to the scientists' camp, where you guys kept showing up to all the time. After that, I tried hard to keep Teegan alive. And I did, until I couldn't help him anymore. At that point in time, I had no choice but to bring him here."

"I'm grateful that you did," Mountain said. "Believe me, I'm very grateful, but now we still have lots of questions, and we need help sorting it out."

She nodded. "You might, but that doesn't mean I have any answers for you."

He laughed. "You're doing fine so far." He gave her a wry smile. "So don't give up on me now."

MOUNTAIN STAYED AT her side, as Amelia napped, then woke. He asked a few more questions, and then she slept some more.

When Magnus came to the clinic at dinnertime, he asked Mountain, "How's she doing?"

"She's doing better, I think. She seems to be getting a little stronger, but she'll be a while yet."

Magnus nodded. "Anything helpful?"

"Not a lot. I keep asking her questions, for descriptions, anything that might shake loose. She remembered that her shooter moved with a lot of grace, as if somebody used to physical activity."

"But that's what we would expect out here," Magnus muttered, with a frustrated tone.

"I know. It doesn't help at all. Anybody who's out here is obviously at a certain fitness level, so that's not getting us anywhere."

"On the other hand, we can't force it, and she can only give us what she can give us, and sometimes that won't be enough." Magnus sighed.

Mountain nodded, commiserating. "I know. I know, and, at the same time, I don't know what else we're supposed to do."

"You could let your brother talk to her."

"I'm planning on it. He's coming in after dinner."

"Oh, good," Magnus said. "In that case, why don't I relieve you, so you can go get yourself some food for a change. If she wakes up again, I'll let you know."

Mountain thought about it and nodded. "Good idea," he agreed, with a hearty smile. "I'll be back in a few minutes."

Knowing that Magnus meant for him to stay and eat in the kitchen and to have a bit of a break, Mountain fully intended to grab some food and come straight back. As he walked into the kitchen, tired and yet relieved to see food, not having been privy to or even caring about the ongoing saga in the kitchen without the chef, Mountain saw Avalon working behind the counters, looking overwhelmed. He smiled. "Still you, *huh*?"

"Me and Chrissy," she replied, with a smile. "We're holding up okay."

"And we're all very grateful that you are," he said.

She laughed. "Everybody wants to know that meals will be cooked by somebody other than them."

"How's Chef holding up?"

The smile immediately fell from her face, and she shrugged. "I take him food, but he doesn't talk. I'm not even sure that he's eating."

Mountain nodded. "After dinner, maybe I can step in and see him too," he offered, fatigue in his voice.

Avalon looked at him and frowned.

He shrugged. "I've been spending most of my time with Amelia, trying to see if she knows anything that we can use to solve this."

"Oh, God," Avalon added, "I hope there is something because I really don't want to believe it was Elijah. He has been the one guy in this place who always had my back. Even when Ralph accused me of poisoning him, and everyone was looking sideways at me, … Chef never did, not once. You need to make damn sure that he really did this because I don't believe it for a second. I just don't see that Elijah could have done any of this."

"I know, and that's how most of us feel, but he's not helping his case at all by staying silent."

"I heard, and I don't understand that either." She shook her head. "You only do that if you're protecting somebody you love." She raised both hands in frustration. Just then somebody else came in to talk to her. She looked over at Mountain, and he quickly moved on, grabbed his food, and headed back to Amelia.

As he walked into the clinic, Magnus got up from behind the desk and announced. "She's still sleeping, honest."

Mountain snorted. "I expected her to still be sleeping. She's been waking and sleeping at fairly regular intervals, usually directly proportional to her pain meds."

"I guess I can understand that too."

"I'm sure you can. She's been to hell and back over all this," Mountain said, as he sat down and pulled a small table close to put his tray on.

Almost as soon as Magnus was gone, Amelia opened her eyes and stared at Mountain.

"Yeah, it's still me," Mountain said cheerfully, "although I do have food this time."

She looked at it with interest. "Some food might be good," she noted cautiously, "but I don't know how my stomach will hold it."

"We can ask Sydney, if you want."

"Is she around? It seems to be pain-meds o'clock to me," she quipped.

"In that case, I'm sure she'll be here any second." Mountain chuckled. "She has this great inner intuition for somebody needing pain meds. Seems she is always nearby when you need her."

Amelia smiled.

Mountain shrugged. "There are a lot worse things to have. It all comes from Sydney's heart, and she'll do everything she can to get you on the mend again. Are you sure you don't want to let anybody know you're alive?"

"I'm not worried for another day or two. I presume that the villagers already know."

"Why would you presume that?" he asked curiously.

She stared at him. "Because they seem to have a pretty good understanding of what goes on here. The locals at the settlement are good about keeping track of their own."

He pushed the table away slightly and looked at her. "Seriously? They are watching the base?"

She frowned at him. "They've talked to Elijah several times about supplies and whatnot, so, yeah. They've talked to a lot of the people here, throughout some of the different exercises you guys have been doing," she shared, with a nod. "So, nobody here is secretive by any means."

"No, of course not." Mountain pondered that. "I wasn't expecting them to be fully aware of what goes on."

"I don't think they are *fully* aware," she clarified. "However, I think that they're quite comfortable with all of you. Maybe too comfortable to let you know all the details they may have gained," she suggested a bit bitterly, "because it seems as if, in some instances, they don't want anything to do with you guys because they understand better than most what is going on here."

He winced at that. "I'm not sure anybody understands what is going on, if we're being totally honest."

"Being totally honest would be good," she declared, "because I don't know who I can trust. I don't really know what I saw, and all your questions make me doubt even that."

"That isn't an issue," he replied. "I just want your impressions, anything you know or even your ideas, to the best of your ability."

"And yet I could be putting a nail in somebody's coffin, when I don't really know anything. Not to mention that it could lead to someone who doesn't even deserve that coffin."

"Somebody shot you two different times," he pointed out. "Therefore, somebody out here did this."

"What if it was one of my own scientists? I did have peers here, and it could be professional jealousy or dozens of other things." Frustrated, she felt compelled to share a counterargument. "Did you consider that?"

He sat back, looked at her, and nodded slowly. "I did consider that, but I presumed," he admitted, feeling foolish for a moment, "that you would have recognized if it was one of them."

She pondered that and then shook her head. "I've asked myself that a dozen times, and yet it always comes back to the same thing. *I'm not sure.* I don't know who it was for sure, and, even bundled up like that, there's really no way to guarantee who it was or who it was not."

"Interesting. So, back to the beginning then. Are you sure it was someone male?"

She pondered that and then nodded. "Yes."

"Okay. Height?"

She looked at him and shook her head.

"You can't tell?"

"Don't know. Didn't have a landmark to compare him to."

"Why don't you answer this," he proposed, a bit careful-ly. "How did your dogs react to him?"

"They were fine. They were happy to meet whoever it was," she replied. "And that confused me too."

"Are your dogs usually aggressive?"

"No, not at all." She shook her head. "We can't have aggressive dogs in sleds or even out on military games and training. Then taking a moment, she added, "Protective, yes, but never aggressive."

"And they didn't seem to get a negative vibe off him at all?"

"No." She shrugged. "However, I've seen lots of people, been around lots of people, and we haven't exactly had any arguments, or raised voices, or any reason for my dogs to be defensive."

"Even after you were shot?"

"I think they were more confused than anything, and, once he let them loose, they were even more confused, but then he took off."

"They didn't follow?"

"No, they didn't follow, but I'm very close to my dogs."

"But they're still animals," he pointed out.

She gave him a ghost of a smile. "Still animals, but they would have stayed with me no matter what," she declared, and he nodded, understanding that loyalty.

"After this trip, will you come back?" he asked.

"I don't know," she replied lightly. "I want to think that having it all screwed up like this doesn't ruin the joy of being up here." She took a moment, and a smile lit up her exhausted features. "I've been coming for years, and I have a good relationship with the villagers because of it," she shared, with a shrug.

"I understood you have family members here."

"Cousins," she clarified, "distant cousins. Funny enough, I didn't even know about them, until we'd been coming here for a while." She smiled again. "It gives me another reason to come back, not that I need one." She turned toward him. "I love being outdoors, and I love being up here."

"No family?"

One eyebrow raised, she asked in a defiant tone, "What do you mean by *family?*"

"It's just a question."

His response calmed her down somewhat. "I have sisters."

"And yet you haven't told them that you're alive."

"Honestly, I don't think I even told them that I came up here. So being alive versus not being alive isn't anything they would be worried about."

"What about text messages and all that?"

"We don't communicate very often. It's usually about birthdays and holidays and that sort of thing," she replied. "They've got three, four kids apiece," she shared, with an affectionate smile, "and they're all very busy with their families."

No rancor was found in her voice, and she sounded perfectly okay with it all. "And you get along with everybody? Is that right? Nobody with any reason to try and kill you?"

She stared at him. "No," she declared, with quiet emphasis. "Nobody there would have any reason to kill me. "Good God, you're a fine one to talk."

"Hey, that's how my mind works," he stated.

"I don't think I like the way your mind works."

He stared at her. "My mind"—he took a moment to orient himself, as if looking for a way to not offend her—"is very aware of humanity and all its weaknesses. Greed is often the biggest." He had to try to soften the blow by some margin. "So, just because somebody tried to kill you up here doesn't mean that the request for that death didn't originate from somebody who may have been in a position to receive more inheritance, if you weren't around to receive it."

She blanched at that. "That's not a nice thought either. … As far as I know, there is no inheritance for me to receive, no money for anybody else to get, and nobody who would profit from my death."

"And yet there was talk about some issues between you and Myles. I heard *Dr. Morrison* was a huge name. Then Anna killed Myles—and John too."

She winced. "As for Myles, he was the kind of guy to write his name on my research papers and not give credit where credit was due," she stated, with a bitter tone. "We've had arguments over it in the past, but it wasn't an issue this time because he isn't on any of my paperwork anyway," she pointed out, with a knowing smile. "Therefore, any problems he might have had with me would be because of my reputation and not so much because of anything that I was doing at this time. Same goes for Anna. John was a bit of wildcard, but he was always fair. So, all this seems to be an exaggeration, if nothing else."

"Since John died a while ago, could Myles have hired somebody to take you out, but then maybe he died before the plan had been executed? Or maybe he heard the plan had been executed," he suggested on second thought, "and then proceeded with the rest of his nightmare, more of a group suicide attempt."

"And yet it was his nightmare, not everyone's."

"No, but that doesn't mean everybody else didn't know about it."

"True," she muttered. "God, that makes all of it sound as if we're some murdering bunch of scientists, doesn't it?"

"Yeah, it sure does," he teased, with a big grin. She

stared at him in disbelief. He cracked a smile. "Hey, I'm making sure I cover all avenues."

"Jesus," she muttered, as she settled back, letting her eyelids drift closed. "You wanted to know the truth, and I will give it to you. Myles was a moron, but he didn't hate me that much."

"Did he hate you at all?"

"I think professional jealousy might have been an issue, and he always wanted to have that reputation, but he just didn't have it and couldn't get it."

"Any particular reason why not?"

"Yeah, he wasn't that good," she stated. "You should know lots of people in your own field, who, in your world, seem to be good soldiers, but you know they aren't that good. They aren't good enough."

"Right," he agreed, "and we have people here to rival your story. Some we had to dig, to find only recently."

"Such as?"

"Our colonel's in trouble."

She looked at him in surprise. "What do you mean?"

"He was tasked to babysit this training session of international teams, after he was disgraced when a rescue mission went sideways. After that, incidents of inappropriate actions were filed, followed by a few more investigations on complaints of inappropriate behavior," he shared. "The colonel came under fire for the charges filed against him, and, though nothing was ever proven, he got some bad marks against him. Thus he was appointed CO here, maybe as a punishment. Since then, things have continued on a downhill slide. So we're wondering if someone has it in for him, making this his last stop in his military career and a humiliating end."

She winced at that. "I would never consider being sent up here a punishment, but, I guess, for other people, maybe it is."

"I can't speak about anyone else. In his case, he's just trying to finish out his career, until he can get his retirement. I'm not even sure how long he's got. For all I know, he could be retiring at the end of this mission. But whenever it is, he's trying to lay low and to get out with his pension and some degree of dignity, then retire in peace and quiet."

"I'm certainly not against that," she said, "as long as he's doing all he can to end whatever nightmare is happening here."

"So, you never felt as if you should come in and say anything to anybody here? Certainly you knew some of the people here."

"Sure, I'd met a few others over time. I finally realized I'd known Magnus a bit from his work on the generator at the scientists' camp. Still, I didn't understand what was going on down here, and it's not as if I wanted to know," she admitted. "I talked to your chef a few times. I kept quiet, and presumably so did he. Honestly it was probably a win-win."

"Not if people were getting hurt," Mountain argued, watching her carefully.

"You mean, dying," she snapped.

"Yeah, that too, but we did manage to save a couple."

"I still don't understand what all this is about," she said.

It brought a gentle smile to his face. "I can fill you in on some of it." Then he explained about the scientists, and Anna's attempt to kill them all with the exhaust from the generator. He told her about Anna killing Myles and John, but that was about love gone wrong. Mountain also briefly filled in Amelia on his visits to the village and Teegan's informal investigation, or some of it. Mountain deliberately kept her in the dark about the issues of drugs, sex, and other scandals within these walls. Joy, Yegorahn, Jerry, and Scott were not her headache. He did explain some about Nikolai and about his father being murdered years ago.

"You think it's related?" Amelia asked.

"We're wondering if it's related," he shared, surprised at how easy she was to talk to and at how natural it felt to be around her. "When you think about it, an awful lot of shit is going on around this place, but it had to come from somewhere. People don't usually start spreading animosity and killing their coworkers."

"Unless they're serial killers," she pointed out. "In which case they can do whatever the hell they want, and nobody will say anything about it."

He stopped and stared. "Surely, you're not suggesting that."

"No, of course not," she said. "Yet, when you think about a scenario that would keep people from complaining or that would allow the killer to do these things unchecked, having nobody watching over them is a big one."

"It is, but it's still not that easy in a military base, with all these people as potential witnesses."

"Yet," Amelia pointed out, "what a perfectly isolated spot with a pool of thirtysomething victims to kill off, left, right, and center, without any reservations."

"But we're not some drunk on the street, we've all got exceptional skills."

"Maybe your killer does too. Maybe, if this is his selected playground, it *is* that easy. Maybe he likes the competition of it all," she countered. "And maybe that's what this person does all the time. Maybe he came up here, hoping to fulfill a fantasy, or maybe hoping that some other idiot would be here, and he could get payback, and maybe that payback involved killing someone and blaming someone else."

Mountain stared at Amelia, as new theories swirled around in his head. "Hadn't considered a few of those ideas," he muttered, with a light chuckle, "but some of them are out there a bit."

"Well, yeah …" She snorted. "Anybody who's doing these things is already pretty far out there, in case you hadn't noticed," she stated, her tone wry.

"Very true," he murmured, "very true."

"And, if you think about it," she added, "whoever is doing this intended to kill up here and planned it ahead of time."

"The trouble is, we did cross-reference a lot of people and their pasts. This is a training base, with participants from various countries. However, this isn't the only survival training base in the world or the only survival session held here either. So, the same people show up at other military bases they have been in, at other missions they have been on, and the like. Everybody really, except for some of the foreign teams here or the newbies, has spent time at the same places as someone else who is also here. The American teams have cross-country mountaineering and survival programs all the time, and that brought on far too many cross-matches to do us any good in singling out a suspect. People at this level are crossing paths all the time, and several of them had met up on other training missions abroad as well, some in Germany, the middle East and even some in Switzerland," he shared. "So, it's not beyond the realm of possibility that some history exists between a lot of people here that is now coming into play."

"There's a history all right," Amelia declared. "Just consider Nikolai's father's death and all the years in between. Maybe Nikolai saw somebody here who might have been related to that scenario."

"We wondered about that. Eric went missing, for several weeks, then returned to the base to kill someone but died himself. Nikolai knew Eric the best of everyone here. Yet Nikolai still couldn't tell us much. Eric wasn't well liked and had his secrets. We were thinking that Eric might have been trying to blackmail someone, but we don't have anybody to point a finger at."

She nodded, as she settled back in her bed. "I'm sure you will," she muttered, with an odd expression. "You have to keep digging deep enough."

"We thought you would have the answers," he stated abruptly.

She widened her eyes and looked at him in surprise. "Me? Why would you assume that? I'm not even part of this base."

"No, but somebody apparently hates you enough to shoot you, intending to kill you, … someone from this base."

"I don't think that they hate me enough to shoot *me*," she clarified. "I think they're scared of me, of what I may have seen, and of what I can do to stop them."

And, with that, she drifted off to sleep, leaving him sitting here, considering all she said.

DAY 5 AFTERNOON

MELIA WOKE UP with a shock and a weird sense of urgency. Shifting gingerly in the bed, she groaned again, as the pain caught her by surprise. "Why the hell is that still so damn painful?" She muttered out loud to no one in particular.

"Maybe because you got shot twice this last time," Sydney stated in her calm, matter-of-fact way. She looked over at Amelia and smiled. "Outside of that pain from waking up, how are you feeling?"

"Better. I'm getting stronger, or at least it feels that way."

"Which is a good thing," Sydney said, with a bright, cheerful smile, "since we still have a lot of our own headaches here to deal with."

"Yeah, maybe," Amelia muttered. "I'm not sure what all this base chaos is about though, so it'll be good if Mountain can go find somebody else to hassle."

Looking at her carefully, Sydney offered, "If you aren't comfortable talking to Mountain, I'm sure I can put a stop to it."

"No, it's not that I'm bothered by it. Sure, it's not pretty, and the fear is always that I've missed something, that I've forgotten something, or that something in my brain hasn't jelled as it should," she admitted, with fear poking at her, "and that's very disconcerting for me. I don't want to think that I know something and can't remember and then have someone else get hurt."

"I get it," Sydney agreed. "However, the bottom line is that, what somebody can know, they know, and what they can't know, they don't. And usually people don't understand that some seemingly unrelated or unimportant little tidbit of information can be very important."

"Oh, I hear you," she said, "but you're not making me feel any better."

Sydney laughed. "Sorry about that, but it is one of the more frustrating aspects of life."

As Amelia lay there, she whispered, "Sydney, … any chance of a coffee?"

That made Sydney smile. She checked her watch. "Maybe so, but I don't want to leave you alone."

"I'm hardly alone, am I?" she asked, with a grin. "How many people are around this place?"

"Thousands." When Amelia's gaze widened, Sydney laughed heartily. "Kidding," she said, with a smile. "In the low thirties, though it varies when we have anybody here delivering supplies and whatnot."

Amelia nodded. "Right, so, what are the chances of anybody coming in here and attacking me, particularly if they don't know whether I'm even alone or not?"

"So far," Sydney began carefully, so as not to alarm Amelia, "we haven't left you alone at all, so you tell me." She hesitated, but then Magnus popped in through the door.

Sydney looked at him with relief, and he smiled that brilliant smile of his. "Your timing is impeccable. Do you think you could sit with her long enough for me to go grab coffee?"

"Sure," he replied, with a smile, as he walked closer to

Amelia.

Staring up at him, Amelia smiled. "Sorry, I was hoping for a coffee, but I didn't realize I needed a nursemaid the whole time. This is a bit too much."

"It's all about keeping you safe."

"I still don't understand why anybody would care about hurting me though."

"You've been shot three times on two different days," he noted, "so it doesn't matter if you understand the shooter's motivation or not. We'll do everything we can to keep you safe, whether you want it or not."

"Of course I want to stay safe," she stated, giving him a hooded gaze. "Why would you even suggest otherwise?"

He shook his head. "I'm not suggesting otherwise, but I've seen a lot of things, while I've been up here, and a lot of things in my life. Sometimes you realize everything isn't always the way it appears."

She nodded. "I can agree with that. … And, sure as hell, whatever is going on in this place doesn't appear to be what it seems either."

He gave her a ghost of a smile. "We are working on it."

"Maybe you can work on it a tad bit … faster, harder?"

"If we could, we would," he stated, "and, as you've seen yourself, we're still looking for information."

"I still don't believe Chef did it," Amelia declared abruptly, her mind caught on the thought that the kind and compassionate chef could be responsible for all the chaos at this base.

"Excuse me?"

"Elijah. … He can't possibly be responsible for this mess."

"No? I gather that is your opinion, and it is one that is

shared by many," he admitted. "However, Elijah's not talking, and, if he won't talk, he's not helping his case or ours."

She went quiet for a moment, then spoke. "So, who's he protecting then?" Startled, he looked at her, and she shrugged. "There's no other reason for him to stay quiet. Somebody close to him must be responsible, and he's either trying to muddy the waters and keep you guys confused or trying to give the other guy a chance to step up and to do the right thing. Whether that other guy does it or not is hard to predict."

Magnus nodded thoughtfully, as he sat here. "Interesting analysis."

"Not an analysis," Amelia corrected. "Just human nature."

"Do you have a lot of experience in that?" he asked her, with a wry look.

"Have you ever worked in academics?" she asked, with a laugh. "Every individual industry has its own issues," she stated, with a deep sigh, "but academia? ... Now that is a world unto itself."

He shrugged. "Can't say I've ever had any exposure to it."

"No higher education?"

"Went straight into the military at a young age," he shared, with a broad grin. "No regrets there."

"And this base has all different branches of the services, doesn't it?"

"It does, but not just the United States is represented here. We have multiple countries involved. I did mention that earlier, but you may have been a little woozy at the time. So, yeah, not just the US military is here."

"Which confuses the issue, since I'm sure you can't get background information on people because of that. Is that an issue?"

"I'm not sure that we *can't* get it. I'm just not sure that we would get as much detail as we would like."

She didn't say anything to that and gave him a hooded glance, wondering what access to information they had and whether it even mattered. "He could just be a serial killer," she stated bluntly, "somebody who takes great delight in causing chaos and confusion and hurting people."

"Maybe, but why? What would this person be like?"

"If they're in the military, you would know better than I do that there are all kinds of opportunities to curb the cravings," she pointed out. "And, if somebody is being kept out of a certain part of it, they don't have access."

"Sure, but that's like saying people can go off half-cocked and cause all kinds of chaos, and that's not true, not on a military base. We have rules and a code of conduct to follow. A person like that would stick out immediately."

"Not completely true, as aren't you all trained to be killers?" she argued. "Yet also not wrong." He glared at her, and she raised her hands in peace. "I get it. You don't want to think that anybody in your profession, in this world that you absolutely love, would do something like that. And I'm not sure that they would. What I am saying is that it's a potential breeding ground for somebody along that line."

Amelia then sighed and added, "Like child predators who put themselves in a position where they can absolutely take advantage of children for their little perverse hobbies—for example, to become a social worker. Those kids have absolutely nobody to protect them from a predator, if that person already knows how to work the system and how to get himself into a place where he can do maximum damage. Not because he wants to do maximum damage, ... but because he wants maximum pleasure for himself. And, in a lot of cases, the predators don't even think about it. It's almost instinctive to put themselves into those kinds of scenarios. It's an awful thing to contemplate, I know ... and bad news for everybody."

"Absolutely, but it doesn't change the fact that, when it comes to predators, they need to have that fix, and yet nobody here," he pointed out, "is getting a regular fix."

"And maybe that's because other people have done something to overturn or interrupt his efforts," she pointed out. "Maybe this is, in a way, so much more complicated, and yet that complication could be a whole lot easier."

He blinked at her in confusion.

She shrugged. "I think, at the end of the day, the answer will be simple, but you're not there yet."

"I'm not there at all," he grumbled, frowning at her. "None of us are there yet, and honestly we were really hoping that you would have some answers."

"I'm not sure why I would have had answers. I've been out in the wilds." She glared at him. "Why would you suggest that?"

"Because you saved Teegan."

"I did, and I tried to save the other one too. ... That didn't work out so well for him."

"And we're sorry about Yegorahn's death too," he told her. "You did your best, and all that effort may well have put you on somebody's shit list."

"May have?" She turned with a wry look in his direction. "How about *definitely did*? Or am I delusional to think so? Do you guys go around shooting random people for fun?"

"Can I presume that's what you're thinking?"

"Somebody may have been doing this for a while."

"That doesn't mean that they've been active the whole time, and, for all you know, they've killed in the past, and, for whatever reason, stopped for a time. Sometimes it happens like that, even with prolific serial killers." Magnus grabbed a pad of paper and a pen off the doc's desk, then sat down and started writing notes.

She laughed. "Oh, come on. I'm sure you guys have shrinks and psychologists all over this."

"We do, and we don't," he said. "We're keeping our investigation fairly low-key at the moment."

"Why? So more people can get killed?" She made no effort to minimize the bluntness of her tone.

He didn't even bother looking up, just continued to write.

When the door to the clinic opened, and Sydney walked back in again, Amelia saw two cups of coffee and sighed happily. "It's funny how the simple things in life can have so much more meaning, especially when doing without."

"The simple things in life are important," Sydney claimed, as she walked over, "particularly when you need a lift mentally, just for healing."

"And yet I'm alive," she noted, "so I shouldn't need any-thing."

Sydney gave her a wry look. "When you feel as if you have a perfect life, you can tell the rest of us how that works," she teased, with a cheerful glance over at Magnus. "Did you come up with something useful to help him out?"

"I don't think so," Amelia replied. "I think he's writing notes to confuse me."

Magnus gave a shout of laughter, as he stood up, then

walked toward them and gave Sydney a hug and a kiss on the top of her head. "I'll be back later." And, with that, he quickly turned.

"Wait," Sydney called out. "You didn't tell me why you came in the first place."

"Doesn't matter," he said, as he kept on going. "Things have changed." And, with that, he was gone.

Sydney slowly turned and frowned at Amelia, carefully watching her. "Do you know what that was all about?"

"No idea," she said honestly. "Hopefully something in our conversation triggered him and made sense to him somehow." She was raw and blunt in her speech now, a feature becoming more and more prominent, as she healed. "There isn't much I can do to help. This is all way beyond me."

"Unfortunately," Sydney added, "it's way beyond most of us."

MOUNTAIN LISTENED TO Magnus, as he relayed the conversation he'd just had with Amelia about serial killers and covering for somebody, and together they contemplated these newest theories. Finally Mountain said, "In a way that does fit. Chef is covering for somebody."

"I know, and, as soon as she mentioned it, I started to put the pieces together, but still we don't know an awful lot."

"And it's the part that we don't know that'll bring this to a complete stop, if we can't get some proof or a confession going."

"So, then we have to look at why that could be." Mountain sat here for a long time, Magnus quiet beside him, both of them letting this new avenue and the latest information roll around in their heads.

Magnus looked over at him and spoke in a careful tone. "The best way might be to trap our suspect in some way."

"Yeah, but that's not likely to happen, and that won't be something that would hold up in court."

"In this case, it won't be a normal court of law."

"I know, but, in that sense alone, it'll be even more of an issue that we need to be extra careful about."

Mountain put his fingers on the notepad for a long time and then said, "I'll go confirm a few things with Amelia." He stood up, still frowning. "How did she look, by the way?"

"Better, much better," Magnus said, with a smile. "Seems she'll pull through this just fine."

Mountain smiled. "That would be nice. She's been a pretty tough cookie, up until now."

"You're the one keeping track of her. Have you told her that?"

He shook his head. "No, not really. I may have been keeping track of her, but she did lose me a couple times, much to my dismay."

"You've also been keeping track of her for other reasons. Maybe you should bring that up too," Magnus suggested. "I'm not sure she would be against it."

"Doesn't matter if she's against it or not," Mountain snapped, his tone harsh as he glared at Magnus. "That is definitely not anything I'm planning on dealing with right now."

"Of course not," Magnus noted, with an eye roll. "You've always got to go above and beyond."

Mountain eyed him wryly. "No, but I don't want to

confuse the issue, not when we have so many people who have been hurt by this."

"And, if we don't put a stop to it, where will it end?"

"That's why we have to look for more history."

"Should we bring Mason in on it?"

"Yeah, I think I'll call him now," Mountain replied. "He's our best shot at finding some history covering many, many years. If there is any, that information would be very helpful—if we could come up with it, especially some related history we could use to force the issue."

"Yeah, good luck with that," Magnus said. "I'll head out to check on supplies and Joe again. Hopefully he's doing better. Sandrine mentioned he's quite the sneak these days, and Sydney let it slip that he came in to get some medication. Painkillers that came in a little bit ago, I guess?"

"Sounds as if you're really worried about Joe."

"I think we all are. And what about that new investigator, Samson?" Magnus asked, turning to look at Mountain. "Something's very odd about him."

Mountain nodded. "Yeah, he's on my radar too."

"But he wasn't even here before, so he can't be involved."

"Maybe he's not involved in that way, but I highly suspect he's got more going on behind the scenes than he's letting on."

"Was he here earlier?" Magnus asked in confusion. "Because, if he wasn't, no way he's involved."

"I don't think he was. However, somebody outside could easily have been involved," Mountain pointed out. "We're already looking for a connection from way before all this training session started, so that isn't such a farfetched idea. We can't ever lose track of the fact that somebody could be pulling strings from afar."

Magnus slowly nodded. "I hadn't really made that leap myself," he admitted, "but you're right. It wouldn't take a whole lot to finesse this from another location, particularly if they'd been in direct contact."

"And, when we talk about direct contact, we don't have any right to check who's been in contact with whom," he shared. "Unfortunately that won't go over well, if we start ripping apart phone records."

"We can do it if we have probable cause," he stated, looking at Mountain carefully. "Yet it didn't help with Eric's phone. Either he had just wiped it before he came to the base to kill one of us or it died or it was wet in the snow too long or something else."

"Right, and we may be close, but we're not quite there yet. Which is why I need to get going, so I can talk to Amelia, Samson, and Mason."

Mountain went to the medical clinic first, wondering how much to say to Amelia, but, when he saw her, he winced to see how quiet and bruised and lonely she looked. "Hey," he said, his voice gentle, as he walked in. "How are you feeling?"

She glanced at him and then looked away. "I'm fine." She gave a careless wave. "Magnus was just here. Are you the next bodyguard?"

He snorted. "I don't make a very good bodyguard."

She gave him a small smile. "I highly suspect you're better trained than all of them."

He shook his head. "No, that's not true. I may just have some uglier experience in some ways."

"I can see that," she noted, "but you're also the one who's here, still hoping I've got answers, right?"

"Of course, and I'm still not convinced that you don't."

Surprised, she looked at him and slowly shook her head. "If you're putting all your hopes into the basket with my name on it," she stated, "you're completely wrong and will be very disappointed."

He smiled. "Maybe. … Been there, done that," he said in a nonchalant tone. "I'm not exactly looking for perfection, but any steps in the right direction would help."

"But I don't know anything."

He sat down across from her, then watched as she picked up the fresh coffee he had brought and had several sips. She was using it to shield her face, something to hide behind, and he understood that because something was going on with her that he still didn't understand. Something was going on, and she was keeping it from him. That was starting to piss him off. But getting pissed off and going in like Godzilla, smashing the very pieces he needed, wouldn't help either. Not when it was obvious that she was already wary.

Finally, as Sydney worked in the corner of the clinic, Mountain decided to be as blunt as Amelia was. He had to try. "Amelia, why did you avoid me all those times out in the great grand north?"

She looked at him from behind her cup, her gaze hooded, and half smiled. "How do you know it was me who was avoiding you?"

"Because I could track you quite easily, but it was also obvious that you were trying to avoid me."

Looking at him in surprise, she asked, "Do you think I don't have a reason? Good God, look at what happened when I couldn't avoid you."

He frowned. "You thought I was the one shooting you?"

She shook her head. "No, never. It wasn't that big of a

person, and I, for damn sure, wouldn't be talking to you if I had any such suspicion."

"Ah, so, for once, my size is a good thing."

"I don't know if it's ever a good thing," she conceded in a careful tone, her gaze still on her coffee. "This world isn't built for people who are different, who are better, bigger, faster, … smarter. It's built for the average person, and the minute you're beyond that, life gets a little hard."

He stared at her for a long moment. "Can you tell me in what way you have experienced that firsthand?"

*W*HEN DID SHE *first see him, based on his size? No. that's not what he's asking.* Amelia studied the massive man in front of her but not with fear. Instead she noted a certain edge of excitement, a certain streak of attraction, neither of which she ever really expected to feel. She had felt it the first time her path had crossed his, both of them walking in the village, stopping her in her tracks. Yet he hadn't shared those feelings, just kept on going, and it had left her confused, disoriented, and struggling. She trashed herself about it for quite a while, calling herself a child needing to grow up, because stuff like that only happened in books.

And yet here she was, still looking at him, wondering what the hell was going on with her hormones. When she was drugged, her body didn't know this was happening. Yet now that she was slowly coming back out of the most acute pain, her body was taunting her, as if saying, *Hey, wake up, wake the fuck up out of that stupor.* Amelia got the message. It was clear and conscious. She wanted to yell at her hormones to tell Mountain to take notice because he was oblivious.

She shifted again to look over at Sydney, who, for all intents and purposes, appeared to be ignoring them. Amelia wasn't fooled. If she so much as coughed a single time, Sydney would be at Amelia's bedside in a heartbeat. Meanwhile Sydney had tuned them out, content to let them do their thing for the moment. Amelia's gaze shifted back to Mountain, who was waiting.

She frowned. "I saw you out there many times, but I didn't know who you were, and I didn't trust you," she replied, trying to answer whatever his question had been. "So, I made sure that I stayed out of your way."

He didn't seem to like that answer.

She continued. "I get it. You're probably used to being the one who has the skills to stay hidden, but, up here, Mother Nature equalizes a lot."

His face cracked into a surprising smile. "Good. I'm glad you had that advantage because, if it wasn't me, it was someone else." Then he took a moment to add, "And obviously both times you got shot, you couldn't escape them either time."

"One of them was really good," she noted. "A couple times I thought he was hunting me, stalking me in a way, but then he disappeared."

"Because he's dead," Mountain stated bluntly. "That was probably Eric, although I don't think he was your shooter. I am sure we have mentioned him to you. He was missing for a long while, then broke into the base, hell-bent on a second attack on Chrissy and Whalen, for some reason—maybe because Eric thought they had seen something. Chrissy had no choice but to shoot him to defend them all."

Amelia winced at that. "*Great.* Did you and Magnus discuss my theory at least?"

"We did, and as theories go, it's definitely possible," he admitted. When she looked at him in surprise, he shrugged. "I'm not saying that Chef is protecting someone, but, if he is, we could use a little more psychology on it than we have currently available."

"I'm sure you have lots of people on staff for that," she said.

He gave her a ghost of a smile. "And yet you've done pretty well, so far."

She shook her head. "I just understand people. Some of them, … as I am sure you would agree, are all kinds of nuts."

He laughed at that. "Yeah, that's a good description of people in general, but you seem to have a larger-than-passing knowledge on serial killers."

"Not really," she argued, as she hesitated, wondering how much to say and then realizing it would probably come out eventually anyway, what with these investigators digging into her background as well. "At one point in time, I dated one. Thankfully he didn't choose me as his next victim, and he was caught before our relationship went too far." She took a deep breath and added, "It definitely made me wary."

His eyebrows shot straight up, as he stared at her.

She shrugged. "I figured you would have found out sooner or later."

He smiled. "We might have heard about it eventually, but it's always nicer when people volunteer information. Then we don't feel that we have to pull teeth to get it from them, at least not all the time."

"What difference does it make?" she snapped, glaring at him, frustrated with herself for mentioning it. "The fact that I had the crappy judgment to go out with this guy shouldn't need to be brought up all the time and leave a negative mark on me for the rest of my life."

"No, of course not," he agreed. "Yet has this mention made your past or future harder?"

She gave him a flat look. "Hasn't made it all that much easier," she pointed out.

With a ghost of a smile, he nodded. "Still, your honesty is appreciated."

"And yet it doesn't make a damn bit of a difference. That's my ugly history and doesn't pertain to anybody else."

"Maybe not," he replied, "but you do have an innate understanding that a lot of people here would not."

"Only because I had to go to his court case, give evidence, plus did an awful lot of research myself," she explained. "I never wanted to end up in that situation again."

"Of course not," he stated, "and thankfully you survived. It seems to have potentially given you a sixth sense of sorts."

"Maybe, or maybe it's just paranoia," she muttered, not giving any quarter nor direction. "If you think about it, it's very easy to think that you know something, but it's just as easy to be wrong. I couldn't take the chance of being wrong again."

"At least it was a long time ago," he murmured, "and you're doing fine now. You've got quite a stellar name built up in your field. You have a lot of respect for the villagers, and they also respect you."

She gave a half laugh. "That's because my great-grandfather was related to several of them," she shared. "I mentioned earlier that I have cousins there, did I not?"

He nodded, and, with that last piece handed to him, it felt almost as if the tumblers fell into place in his head.

She nodded. "So, technically, … yes, I'm related to several of them," she said, now coherent and compliant, "but I really don't think you could call that a relationship or a family. My father used to come up on a regular basis and be with the villagers, and he's the one who taught me most of what I know about survival in this place. I just call it my community."

"I can see that."

"He's also the one who instilled the love of this area in me," she added, with a nod. "He sent me to university so I could study and understand the beauty of it." The tears collected in the back of her eyes, as she thought about it. "Definitely some times in my life have been much better than others, and those times up here with my great-grandfather, grandfather and my father were definitely some of the best."

"Anybody else in your family show any interest in the Arctic?" he asked.

With a ghost of a smile in his direction, she shook her head. "No, my sisters prefer not to acknowledge that blood in their lives," she shared. "For me, it's not the blood that matters. It's the people."

Mountain saw the fierceness that he liked so much in Amelia.

"I couldn't care less whether people like my heritage or not," she stated, with a cool look in his direction. "I can tell you that what they taught me was invaluable, and it has kept me alive on more than one occasion, when I've been doing research up here. It's also allowed me to stay out almost indefinitely, looking after myself, and that's how I managed to look after Teegan too," she related.

"Of course. You must have certain skills, and those types of skills are best taught by the elders," he noted. "So it was an easy assumption on our part. We just didn't know the details."

"The details are simple," she said. "I had family who taught me skills and lessons that I chose to learn and to learn well, not like a lot of people in this world who think it's more of a joke than anything,"

"That is understandable too."

"Yeah, it is. Once you need those skills, it isn't something you fool around with," she murmured. "When a need becomes one of survival, there isn't any doubt as to the viability of the information you've spent a lifetime learning."

"And, in your case, you were gifted with that information." He gave her a searching gaze. "That makes it even more valuable."

A GENTLE SMILE whispered across her face, before she even had a chance to hold it back. Something was very comforting about him. She had expected some judgment from him, as she experienced from many others, but none appeared on his face. It was too early to tell, and she was no longer a good judge of men. Maybe she could judge humanity better, but, when it came to individual men themselves, she always questioned everything.

She looked around. "My heritage did cause a problem, when several of the other members at the university found out I had Inuit blood in my family. I certainly won't downplay how unpleasant that was to go through."

He slowly nodded his head. "I'm sorry about that. I don't imagine that would have been fun."

"No, it sure wasn't," she murmured. "Particularly when there was absolutely no need for it, but so much of the academic world is very dog-eat-dog, which is so sad because, again, there is no need for it. I'm here for the work, for the results. I'm not here for the glory. Lots of people don't believe that. They think it's not possible to want one but not the other, and I think that's sad for them. There is so much more to life than being out there, trying to backstab everyone on the climb to the top."

"I'm sorry you had to deal with that prejudice." He nodded. "I've experienced it a time or two in my world as well. My size generally causes other people to stay quiet, rather than pushing it too far," he shared, with a laugh.

With a wry look in his direction, she nodded. "You have that advantage. I didn't. And I'm female to boot, so that's another knock against me."

"Not a knock against you at all," he argued. "Honestly, you've done more out here than I think anybody else on this base could do."

"Except for one," she corrected, with a bitterness to her tone. Mountain raised one eyebrow. She nodded. "The man who shot me."

MOUNTAIN THOUGHT ABOUT her words in the hours that followed. Amelia had been open and honest and had in no way cut back or minimized the effect of her heritage, even though she didn't physically show any signs of it. He'd taken a few hits on his own heritage over the years, but, as he'd explained to her, they were not hits that most people cared to push because of his size alone, and he was okay with using his size when it came to those things that he had no control over.

He had no time or energy for assholes who would judge or knock people for their heritage. There was too much else in this world to spend time on that actually mattered, and he chose not to waste time on those people. Absolutely nothing in her speech, her mannerisms, or her tone suggested that her words were anything but honest and truthful, and, for that, he was grateful. There was no denying the attraction building within him, and finding out they shared similar experiences related to heritage, plus a love of the world and its beauty, certainly didn't hurt either. Yet it was crappy timing, and right now his focus needed to be entirely on solving the rest of this mess going on around them.

As he stopped by the office Samson was using, Mountain poked his head in to see the new investigator standing in the middle of the room, an odd look on his face. Mountain quickly stepped in, closed the door, and announced his presence. "What are you thinking about?"

Startled, Samson turned and looked at him, then frowned, but remained silent.

Mountain frowned right back. "You'll have to share your thoughts sometime," he muttered.

"Will I?" Samson asked, with a note of amusement.

Mountain rolled his eyes, stared back at him, and replied, "Yeah, you will."

"I'm thinking about what Amelia said." Looking down at the notes Magnus had written and handed over to him, he continued, "If she's right, we could be looking for somebody who's potentially been doing this for a long time, someone who stopped permanently for whatever reason, or stopped temporarily and then was triggered to start again."

"It's the triggering to start again that's got me worried," Mountain declared, "because what would it take for that to happen?"

"You would have to look at what had stopped it in the first place," he pointed out. "I've touched base with a couple psychologists and several other specialists in the field, and generally what stops a serial killer can be a change in environment, such as incarceration, where they got caught for a different crime. Sometimes starting a family, having children, can completely change how a serial killer would view his hobby at that point in time. Any big change in life, getting a certain amount of recognition for something he did that's not connected to his hobby but provides that same high. It could be all kinds of things," Samson muttered. "The bottom line is that a serial killer is classed as somebody who's killed three or more people, and, of course, there's a special class for shooters who take out people in masses. However, for a serial killer in this case, we would be looking at somebody who had systematically, slowly murdered people throughout his active period."

Mountain absorbed that for a moment. "Yet we had fires here, plus the generator problems on base and at the scientists' camp, which may or may not be related. We had poisonings, but one was misguided love. We definitely had drug problems on this base. What I'm saying is that, we may well have one serial killer, but we also have others endangering our lives. So we have someone who could also methodically trigger other people to commit crimes, like some cult leader, and he would stay in the shadows. … Yet why? And why now?"

"Sometimes for no other reason than simply because they can. As Amelia mentioned, the military is a hell of a breeding ground for anybody looking for killing opportunities," Samson replied, with a shrug. "Not everybody is geared to kill just for the thrill of it. Some military leaders are absolutely terrified of the destruction they cause when they give orders, particularly controversial orders. Yet other leaders are absolutely enthralled with making decisions that represent life or death to other various people."

They discussed the possibilities for a few minutes, exchanging what they thought on the issues, and then, out of the blue, Samson added, "I'll need to talk to her myself."

Mountain nodded. "I want to be present."

His eyebrows shot up, as he looked back at him. "I want to see how she handles being questioned by somebody else, changes in mannerisms, things such as that," Samson explained.

Mountain nodded. "I have seen her reactions to me, but you could be the wild card."

"I'm fine with that," Samson stated, with a grunt.

"When do you want to do it?"

"Now would be good." Samson shrugged.

"You need to be aware that we spoke about her briefly dating a serial killer, and that is partly why she has so much knowledge and insight into them. Fearful of repeating the experience, yet wanting to understand, she did a lot of studying on the topic."

"You would have thought that might send her into that field, not up here dealing with the mountains and the winter glaciers," Samson noted. "That's a very specialized field in itself."

At that, Mountain explained about her father and great-grandfather. "I wonder if maybe she spent an awful lot of time up here in order to help her recover from dating a serial killer, then later after the deaths of her great-grandfather and her father."

Samson nodded. "That would make sense. She's been blessed to have that kind of training, that kind of help."

"That's what I told her," Mountain confirmed, with a smile. "I'm not sure she believed me, but I sensed relief that I didn't judge her for her Inuit background. She seems sensitive to that."

Samson laughed. "You're the last person to judge her for that or anything else. I'm sure you've got your own horror stories to share."

"I've certainly got a few, but they didn't last very long. People have to be half suicidal to take me on, particularly after insulting me."

Samson nodded and gave a light chuckle. "I can imagine that much. Let's go see what we can rustle up this time," he muttered.

"I've got some contacts looking into the history on various people here to see how much might have come up in background checks that was common or shared among everyone here. We do have chaos going on, with multiple avenues to cause problems or to obscure the main problem. However, what if the killings alone are just by one person?"

"I suspect that it is just one person," Samson declared. "While we have one person in custody, he won't talk, and he hasn't given me any idea as to why he would poison Teegan. Still, that's got to be considered. If Chef's protecting somebody, then he probably knows who the serial killer is. That's what bothers me."

"Not that I think Chef is our serial killer, yet a serial killer would do the same thing—not talk, not explain— wouldn't he?" Mountain asked.

"Maybe, maybe not. Again I've got the shrinks on that too." Samson picked up a notepad, walked to the door, and looked over at Mountain. "Are you coming?"

"Oh, I'm coming," he said, with a smile, "if for no other reason than to see how she reacts."

"You seem to be expecting some reaction," Samson pointed out. "I'm not sure that's being fair to her."

"There is no *fair* right now," Mountain stated. "She seems to be telling the truth. And I, just like her, don't trust that easily."

"Did you date a serial killer too?" Samson asked, with a smirk.

"Nope, but, like her, I also know what people are capable of."

Samson gave him a hard look and nodded. "Don't we all. … Don't we all." And, with that, the two men walked out and headed to the medical clinic.

DAY 5 NEAR DINNERTIME

A MELIA OPENED HER eyes to find Mountain staring at her. She jolted in surprise and shuddered in pain. A second man stared at her, with an open and yet friendly interest. She immediately pegged him as the investigator. She knew someone had to be coming soon, although something was different about him. "*Great*," she mumbled. "More questions?"

"Always more questions," Mountain replied cheerfully. Then he frowned and stared at her intently. "How are you feeling? Do you need more pain meds?"

"I've felt better," she muttered bitterly and shifted slowly in the bed. In spite of her best efforts, a groan escaped. She stilled and lay here, her eyelids closed for a minute to catch her breath.

"Sorry," the investigator replied in an apologetic tone. "Some things can't wait."

She gave him an easy look and nodded. "Some things can wait. Some things shouldn't have waited," she muttered.

"Meaning?"

"I don't know. It feels very much as if everything you're doing is too little, too late."

"That's how we all feel," Samson admitted. "We're hoping to stop another death, but we're also hoping to bring somebody to justice. As I'm sure you've already guessed, I'm

Samson, one of two investigators here. It's nice to meet you."

"I wish I could say it was nice to meet you but, under the circumstances, not so much. For the record, I don't think it's about justice." She paused for a long moment. "It feels very much as if something else is going on here, and it's freaking scary."

"I won't argue with you on that one," Samson said, as he pulled up a spare chair.

She looked around and realized that Sydney was gone. "This must be an intense questioning session, if you kicked Sydney out," she noted, focusing her attention on Samson.

"I didn't kick her out," he corrected, with a smile. "She's gone to get you some coffee."

Her heart lightened at the idea, and a smile touched her face. "Coffee would definitely help." She turned her head to the side to have a better vantage point and to be a bit more comfortable. "It'll be really nice to get out of here at some point."

"It will be nice, but still better if we can get everybody out in one piece," Samson explained. "Otherwise I'm afraid nobody's getting out."

"Including me?"

"Including you," he confirmed.

She let her eyelids drift closed. "How are my dogs?"

"They're fine," Mountain replied, with a chuckle. "I check on them every day."

A glimmer of a smile crossed her lips. "My dad would have my head if I didn't look after those dogs."

"I would probably do the same," Samson agreed. She looked at him, and he nodded. "Yes, Mountain told me about how you dropped off your dogs with Joe first, if that's what you're wondering."

"Any particular reason why you need that information?" she asked cautiously.

"I happen to think the good guys love and respect animals. So for you to get them to safety, before you got yourself to the doc, tells me a lot about you. Plus, I let Joe know where you were, how you were, to ensure we were all on the same page," Samson shared, with that same careful tone. "Is it a problem?"

She shrugged. "No, not really. I'm not planning on sticking around here. My dogs and I will return to the village as soon as I can. So it really doesn't matter either way."

He gave her a ghost of a smile. "Even though you are not military, you are welcome here, for as long as you like or for as long as it takes you to heal. I have absolutely no problem with your heritage," he told her. "Anybody who does is an idiot."

She stared at Mountain, her gaze hard. "A lot of idiots are out there," she stated, peeling her gaze away from Mountain, then staring at Samson under a hooded gaze. "Generally they come in the form of all kinds of military."

"I come from the navy," Samson stated, "and we have our fair share of idiots too. Thankfully you won't meet too many of them here."

"I wonder," she noted, with a slight tilt of her head.

"Do you think you were shot both times because of your bloodline? You certainly don't visibly carry your heritage," Samson shared. "So unless you tell somebody …"

"I guess it depends on if *you'll* tell somebody."

"Me?" He looked at her, with an expression of astonishment. "Why would I do that? I'm here to sort out something completely different. I couldn't care less where you come from or who you spend your holiday time with. Honestly,

I'm jealous that you had family like that to call your own."

"That's all I had though," she clarified. "My sisters and I aren't close, and they didn't have anything to do with that side of the family, and we still tend to disagree over them, even after they have all died."

"That's what family is all about though." Samson grinned. "You get to disagree with them, yet still live your own life and make your own choices."

She smiled. "Agreed. As for the matter at hand, I really don't think I can add anything else to what I've already told Mountain and Magnus."

"I'm not so sure about that. So we'll keep moving forward and see what comes up."

"Ask away then," she muttered, as she settled into her bed. "Honestly, I can't remember anything else to tell you."

He looked down at his notes. "I understand you saw whoever it was shooting at you each time."

"No," she corrected. "I saw several people out there several times."

"Was the shooter with others, or was the shooter alone?"

"The one guy I thought was stalking me, which may or may not have been for fun," she replied, as an afterthought, "was alone."

Samson looked at Mountain, who mouthed, *Eric.* Then Samson checked his notes again. "No dogs were with the shooter?"

She shook her head. "No dogs. He was on skis, and honestly, he was moving at a hell of a clip. So it was somebody used to these Arctic conditions or who has spent a long time working in these conditions. In other words, it wasn't a hardship for him to be out there, unlike many other people on base."

"Got it." Samson nodded, as he wrote down more notes. "You couldn't tell his age or anything? You couldn't tell more by his posture, the way he moved, anything?"

"No, I couldn't tell any of that. I'm not sure anybody could, honestly, in that white camo winter gear." She frowned, as she thought about what she had seen and how he'd moved. "He seemed relaxed. He wasn't awkward out there. His movements were natural, and he seemed happy being out there."

"But you only ever saw the one person."

"No," she clarified, forcing her point again. "I saw lots of people. You have a lot of training going on." She took a moment to add, "Depending on the time of day, day of the week, and weather conditions, I saw quite a few people, but nobody who I felt comfortable enough with to bring any of your missing people back to the base."

"What about Teegan Rode?" Samson asked.

"When I first found Teegan, he was in a rough shape, and I didn't want him traveling, not until I could get him a little more stable," she explained, "and then I got shot the first time. I did move him and me to another ice cave, where I had more supplies—food, water, blankets—where we and the dogs could lay low for a few days. However, after the second shooting, I couldn't do any more for Teegan. I needed help for him and for me."

"You did what you could, and we thank you for looking after Teegan and Yegorahn," Samson stated in a firm tone. "Nobody blames you for that."

"Just me," she muttered bitterly. "At least Teegan's okay, although you guys are apparently keeping him away from me. In case there is any confusion on the matter, I very much want to see him."

"He's asked several times to see you," Mountain admitted. "I just … I didn't want you upset."

"Why would seeing him upset me?" she asked, astonished.

He gave a ghost of a smile. "I don't know for sure. I was just following my instincts."

"Don't follow that one anymore," she quipped. "It's totally fine, and I would very much like to see him, particularly if he's up and walking and doing better. I just have to see it with my own two eyes."

"I can assure you he is up and around, doing much better."

"In that case, I definitely want to see him. You've got questions, well, so do I," she stated, with a headshake. "The only time he was really coherent, I asked him what happened to him. However, everything he said was a jumble, telling me it wasn't safe here on base, and I didn't dare bring him back. He kept blabbing about how he would be killed. Honestly, seeing him like that? … I didn't know what to do. I thought about it for a while. I finally decided that I would get him healthy enough, so either we could come back here together or he could carry on and make that decision on his own. I really didn't want to make that call for him."

"We certainly appreciate your keeping him alive," Samson repeated, with that same smile. "Do you have specific memories of the things he said while he was in your care?"

She winced. "Everything he mentioned was pretty crazy," she murmured. "It's not as if anything made any sense."

"By *anything*, you mean?"

"Anything, everything. He was talking about not being safe. He was talking about how a killer was on the base. He mentioned talk of betrayal and all kinds of stuff. Honestly, it had the makings of a great thriller story, but I was missing the punch line. I was missing the plot, and I sure as hell didn't know who the boogeyman was, and that was the most bothersome point of all."

Samson remained passive and didn't say anything, his face masked.

Amelia continued. "Without knowing who the bad guy was, how could I dare bring Teegan back in? I couldn't hope for the best with some naïve, optimistic attitude. That wouldn't work for me. Knowing what I know now, I probably didn't make the right decision in keeping him out there. However, at the time, with the limited information I had, it was the only choice I felt good about. I knew that, as long as I could keep him warm and could let his body begin to heal, then maybe I would have a chance of figuring out what was wrong here. I, for sure, didn't want to turn over Teegan to the guys who had tried to kill him in the first place," she muttered. "In the end, that didn't work out so well for either of us, and I ran out of options."

"Actually it worked out better than you can imagine," Samson stated, giving her a calm and steadying smile. "Believe me, we are very grateful for all the help you provided to Teegan and now sharing this information with us. From what I understand, Teegan would never have survived without you."

"Maybe so, but it doesn't seem that I was any help at all," she muttered in frustration. "As a matter of fact, all of this feels terribly wrong."

"Because?"

"I feel as if I should have gotten more information from him, as if I should have had something to go by, and instead … it feels as if it was such a betrayal to bring him back," she admitted, the words flowing out, as she realized just how much it had all bothered her. "Here is this guy depending on me to keep him alive, and then I got shot, the second time. Nothing I could do but turn him over to the very people who had likely tried to kill us both in the first place," she cried out.

Seeing her getting so upset, Mountain jumped up, walked over, and wrapped his massive arms around her.

She hated that the shaking had already begun, but it had, and, by the time she calmed down, after releasing that load of guilt, Mountain's expression was stern. "Look. You did the best you could. You did everything you could, which was far more than most people would or could have done," he declared, stressing his point. "Please stop beating yourself up over it."

She gave him a ghost of a smile. "Tough love, *huh?*"

"If I thought tough love would work, I would be all for it. But, in this case, you've got to stop blaming yourself. You saved Teegan. I know you saved him because I was out there looking for him … the whole time."

"So why didn't I trust you enough to give him to you then?" she asked in confusion, wondering why she couldn't trust anyone with Teegan. "I certainly saw you enough. You and Chef. I saw him out there with several other people. All kinds of people were out there." She sighed and dropped her head to the side. "With dogs, without dogs, lots of people were outside traveling around, including you. I saw you, … but I didn't trust you enough to bring in Teegan."

He nodded, then looked over at Samson, who studied her intently.

Samson asked, "When you say you saw Chef Elijah out there, do you know him?"

"I had met him several times, when survival ops were going on here, while I was gathering data. For this training period, having found Teegan early on, I'd watched Chef for a while, learning his habits. Then I waited until after dark, after the dinner rush, when I was pretty sure he would be alone in the kitchen here on base. In fact, he liked to feed leftovers to the dogs at night, so I approached him outside, told him that I was in trouble and needed supplies."

Both Samson and Mountain were on the edge of their seats, as if she were about to open the door to Valhalla.

"He literally opened up the back door and told me to take what I needed, and, for that, ... believe me, I'm very grateful. I didn't do it often, but, once I had Teegan to look after," she admitted, taking a deep breath, "it got a bit harder. I also managed to get a few medical supplies and other things, which made a huge difference. I know Chef wasn't supposed to be helping me, but honestly he's a good guy, and I can't believe he has done what you guys are saying he's done."

"Not sure he has either," Samson agreed.

"Then maybe that's part of the problem. There's that sense ... of frenzy, a sense of ... finality."

"An ending, you mean?" Samson asked, with a questioning gaze.

"I guess that's what I mean." She shrugged. "I don't know. Something my father used to tell me all the time was to listen to the words in my head, yet not so much the words themselves but the feelings attached to them. He would tell me that so many of the answers we need in this world, we already know, but we don't listen closely enough to what our hearts and our minds are telling us."

Samson studied her, then slowly nodded. "I would agree

wholeheartedly with that sentiment. Sounds to me as if you were blessed in many ways to have such a good man in your life."

She nodded. "I absolutely was. You don't realize how much you need your family, want them, rely on all the information they give you, until they're gone." She shook her head, saddened by the memory of her loss. "Losing my great-grandfather was hard, but losing my father was … devastating," she murmured, and then, as if shaken out of a stupor, she held her head high. "Yet they both died in their sleep, happy with their lives, satisfied that they had lived to the best of their ability in peace with the world around them. I could only hope for half as much when I go," she whispered, "but I sure as hell don't want to go because some asshole put a bullet in me."

At that, Samson laughed. "And we don't want that to happen either, which is why you're still under guard, why your presence here is still being kept quiet, all while we track down every detail we can. I don't suppose you remember anybody else you saw out there."

"I saw lots of people," she replied in frustration, then pointed to Mountain. "I already told him most of it. Sometimes people were alone and drifting, groups too. Sometimes groups of threes, and sometimes with these long rifles. I'd never seen them before, but I don't know much about the military equipment you guys have here anyway."

"Go on then. Any description helps."

"Okay, … sometimes that white camouflage gear blends in so damn perfectly that it's hard to see people and becomes more about looking past that and understanding the movement." Then she frowned. "One time … he almost saw me that day."

"What do you mean? Who? When?"

"I was outside one day, before I ever got shot," she said a bit forcefully. "I was in one of my ice caves, … checking my data readings because I wasn't sure what was happening. Some of the data appeared to be wrong, and I wasn't happy that the meters might not be working properly." She took a moment to collect her thoughts. "You would think that the meters are conditioned for that level of cold, but they're really not," she explained, with an apologetic shrug. "Anyway, I was hunched down around the ice cave, when I heard a sound and froze—because one of the first things you're taught is not to move, right? It's the movement that catches the eye, and this guy was moving quickly. He didn't appear to see me, and he was heading north at a fast pace. However, I was close by. I would say only five meters away from him. I froze and didn't do anything, not until he was gone."

"You didn't say hi? You didn't reach out to him in any way?"

She winced. "God no. Absolutely nothing inside me made me think for even a second that I should reach out and talk to this guy. He was clearly on a mission, and he was heading after something—or someone. Honestly I thought it was one of your war games again because somebody was ahead of him, and it looked as if he was prepping for a shot. One of my dogs made a sound at that point, and he shifted, he turned. I have no idea what happened, so maybe he saw me. Maybe he didn't. I don't know. He didn't like something anyway, and he took off." She shrugged. "I figured maybe it was lucky for the guy he was chasing."

"Any idea who the guy was?"

"Elijah," she stated, "at least I figured it was Elijah. Not too many people are his size either." She looked over at

Mountain intently. "It definitely wasn't you, and I'm thinking now that maybe this was before you ever got here. You're bigger than he is, … but still, Chef's built like a bazooka."

"Elijah is big," Mountain agreed.

"And you're saying he was out there ready to shoot someone?" Samson asked.

"No, no, no," she denied urgently. "Elijah was the one out there about to get shot." Both men exchanged a look and then turned back at her. "I figured it was part of your war games, the training missions or survival ops or whatever. Are you saying it wasn't?" she asked, bewildered.

"Elijah does ski for the fun of it, but he doesn't participate in our war games," Mountain muttered. "I don't think he ever went out on any of the training missions."

"And yet he could," Samson noted. "He's still military, and he's still required to get in some survival training. He's part of the team, particularly if he chose to be here. So, if it was before we got here, maybe he was out there, taking part in a war game. Not to mention the fact that he could have requested it," Samson added.

"That's another question to go ask him then," Mountain noted, looking at Samson. "And, if he was the one out there, and he wasn't there for any war games, why would somebody want to kill him?"

"That is a very good question."

LEAVING AN EXHAUSTED Amelia in Sydney's capable hands, Mountain and Samson immediately headed down to talk to their incarcerated chef. Elijah looked up, settled deeper into his chair, his arms crossed over his chest, and remained silent.

Mountain sat across from him, holding up a hand to him. "Elijah, … nobody here believes anything that's been rumored about you," he began carefully, "or whatever's been implied. Those of us tasked with the job to try and prove it, are trying to prove you had nothing to do with it." He caught the surprise in the older man's gaze and nodded.

"You're very well liked here, and people don't want to believe that you had anything to do with any of this," he muttered. "Trouble is, … it doesn't seem you're terribly interested in clearing your name or pointing the finger at whoever is responsible for this shit." Chef's lips curled at that, and Mountain nodded. "By that look, … I understand. I do. We all make friends here. We all have favorites. For all I know, you spawned a daughter, who nobody knows about, and somebody here raped her, and you decided on some payback. Of course this is a very convoluted way to go about that, and I don't see it, but, hey, we have to consider everything."

At that, Elijah snorted at him. "You guys really are grasping at straws, aren't you?"

"Of course we are," he replied in a desperate tone. "You know that too because a group of us is trying to prove you're innocent, and another group of us is trying to prove you're guilty." He took a moment to gauge Chef's reaction, then added, "Nobody wants to believe you're guilty, but we need answers one way or another. We *need* answers, Elijah."

"It doesn't matter what the answers are," he said, his tone gloomy. "I'm guilty."

Mountain pounced on his words. "Okay, but guilty of what?"

Elijah looked down, as if angry at himself for giving Mountain anything to go on.

"Whatever it is, … it appears it could be a completely different thing. We understand you helped Amelia."

He nodded slowly. "Yeah, I'm definitely guilty of that, and I would do it again too. It's not as if she was hurting anyone, and clearly she needed a hand. I didn't know that she was trying to keep Teegan alive at the time, but I'm certainly not sorry I helped her, … even if it wasn't for Teegan."

"It was for Teegan and for the other man, Yegorahn," Mountain confirmed in a sad tone. "I'm sorry she couldn't keep the other one alive, but I'm grateful that you helped her. For Teegan's sake, I'm grateful."

Elijah nodded.

Mountain studied him carefully. "So, no matter what anybody here says about that aspect of it, you'll always have my thanks."

At that, Chef didn't say anything right away, but he seemed to relax a bit. "So, the rumors have to do with a whole lot more?" Chef asked.

"Murder, death, payback, God only knows," Mountain shared. "Too many factors are involved that we can't quite sort it all out. Amelia is doing much better by the way, and, with any luck, she'll pull through, if we can keep whatever asshole here who's after her from making a third attempt."

"A third?" Chef asked, startled.

Mountain looked at him and nodded slowly. "Yes, a third. She was shot the first time in the shoulder, but managed to deal with it herself, even while caring for Teegan and living off the land by that time. She was doing all right and was managing with Teegan, but then, when she was shot later, more recently, twice this time, she knew she was in trouble and couldn't look after him and herself. Somehow she managed to get Teegan here, believing she had to take the risk or he would surely die anyway. So, she saved him by delivering him to us, then went back to the tundra and tried to survive on her own. In the end, she couldn't control her bleeding, and it's nothing short of a miracle that she managed to get herself back here, or she wouldn't have survived. Frankly, while she is doing better, she's definitely not out of the woods because she's lost so much blood."

"Jesus," Chef muttered, "some people are made of steel."

"That is quite true, and she's definitely one of them," Mountain agreed, with a smile. "Thankfully Teegan was the beneficiary of her strength and cunning. She also told us about something she saw some time back. She was able to identify you as one of the parties involved, since she knows who you are because you helped her."

Elijah shrugged and didn't say anything, as if expecting Mountain to continue.

"She didn't realize it at the time, but she had inadvertently interrupted somebody lining up a shot to kill you," Mountain shared and then watched him closely.

At that moment, Elijah turned, startled, and then slowly shook his head.

Mountain nodded. "Yes, it's true." Then he provided the circumstances and the location. "I immediately told her that she had the wrong person, that you mostly stayed indoors and haven't participated in the war games and the survival training here that I knew of, but she is adamant it was you because she had already seen you multiple times outside, and her surety is merit enough. She has also pointed out what we already know, which is how we come to identify people by their size, posture, and movement, since we're typically all dressed the same out there. She is certain it was you, and I believe her."

He winced and nodded. "That's correct. She saw me several times, skiing, feeding the dogs treats outside. … Once I realized she needed help, I would regularly take out some foodstuffs for her." He dropped his head, and they couldn't see his face. "We had a system, a specific date and time. I would leave some leftovers, some canned goods. If for any reason she couldn't make it soon enough, everything would freeze, and the cans would explode anyway. However, that didn't happen very often," he noted, with half a smile.

"She didn't even tell us about that part," Mountain shared, with a glimmer of a smile. "Even now she's trying to protect you."

"There is no protecting me," he stated with finality, and yet a note of sadness filled his tone that made both Mountain and Samson stop and look at him in surprise.

"I don't understand," Mountain said. "Something is here. You know something—something that would make a lot of sense if you would explain it, but, for whatever reason, you're determined not to."

"Yeah, I am determined not to. No benefit to be had in my telling anybody anything, so you can forget that idea."

"Look. Somebody already tried to kill you once that we know of. Now that we've got you locked up in here, like a duck on a pond, for all we know, we've given you a death sentence, and we didn't even mean to."

"Doesn't matter whether you did or not," Chef muttered. "In many ways that will probably be better."

"Whoa, whoa, whoa," Mountain said, "that's not making any sense."

"None of this makes sense," Samson agreed. "The only thing that makes sense is that you're protecting somebody."

Instantly Elijah stiffened and glared at them.

Mountain nodded slowly. "Amelia suggested that you were probably protecting somebody, but we couldn't for the life of us figure out who or why."

"It's not supposed to make any sense," he snapped. "That's just life. Sometimes it makes sense. Sometimes it doesn't. And sometimes it just is what it is, and sometimes it's a whole lot more."

Mountain stared at Chef in surprise. "So, for whatever reason, you don't want anybody to find out who you're protecting or why, and you're willing to take a death sentence for it?"

Elijah shrugged. "She's wrong anyway. I don't remember any time that I would have been in a position to be shot like that. She's mistaking me for someone else."

"No, … she's not," Mountain argued adamantly. "You were in the crosshairs, and, if it hadn't been for a noise made by one of her dogs, causing the shooter to take off, you would have been another mysterious casualty of this military base."

"Whatever." Elijah gave a wave of his hands. "You're grasping at straws, throwing out a bunch of possibilities and seeing if you can get something to stick. I know how you guys work." He sent a hard look in their direction. "Besides, the life we live up here puts us in touch with some very strange bedfellows."

"Now that is very true, Elijah," Mountain admitted. "And I'm wondering which one of them would be upset enough with you to want to do that."

Again Elijah shrugged, but an odd look was in his gaze.

"I'm afraid it's the person you're trying to protect," Samson suggested, "as if whatever deal you've made is about to become no deal for some reason, or he needs some insurance or something." Samson had a specific ring in his tone and with his choice of words.

Mountain looked over at Samson, who studied Chef's face intently.

"Definitely you're concerned about something," Samson stated, "and we'll be more than happy to try and keep you alive, if you're afraid of repercussions. Obviously though you'll have to start talking to us—and soon."

Elijah gave him a genial smile. "You boys go off now. You've got better things to do than sit here and talk to me."

"Better things like what?" Mountain asked.

He looked at him and shrugged, his posture relaxed. "A lot of people are still here, and a lot of people could come to harm," he pointed out. "You don't want that."

"No, I don't want that to happen to you or to anyone else," Mountain said. "I especially don't want anything to happen to Amelia, not after everything she did to help my brother," he added. "And, if you know anything about that, I would appreciate some answers. It might help us save Amelia, Teegan, and you, as well."

"Don't know nothing about nothing," Elijah muttered, taking on a bored tone.

That hit Mountain hard. Starting to feel the fury building within him, he stood up and looked over at Samson. "I'll step out for a few minutes," Mountain stated, his words harsh and his expression ominous.

"Maybe go get some coffee," Samson suggested.

Mountain nodded curtly and walked out without saying a word, as it was all getting to be a bit much. With coffee on his mind, he went to the kitchen. Several women worked away, and, while he was sorry that everything had become such a shit show, he appreciated the fact that they had stepped up. One of the women looked up at him, shoved a cinnamon bun in one of his hands and a cup of coffee in the other, then shooed him away.

He looked down in surprise and then smiled, as she continued to carry on, as if that were an everyday occurrence. Maybe it was. Maybe that was the world they lived in now.

As he stepped outside for a moment of much-needed fresh air, he realized how much of an advantage Chef had, the entire time that he was here. He had vantage points, both inside and out, that allowed him to watch things going on all the time. He could keep an eye on people, if he chose, including the kid who had worked for him. The thought of Scott stepping outside stirred up something inside Mountain, and he didn't like it one bit. He frowned, wondering if Elijah would have had anything to do with Scott's death.

With his cinnamon bun eaten, but his coffee in hand, he walked back to where Samson still spoke with Elijah. Mountain stepped in and looked at Chef, getting right in his face. "Did you kill Scott, that young kid who worked with you?"

A sorrowful look crossed Chef's face that he schooled right away, then immediately shook his head. "No, Scott was a hell of a good kid," he replied in a hard tone. "I would never have done that."

"I can't imagine that you did any of it. Even asking if you did or didn't seems wrong in the first place," Mountain stated, as the tightly wound coil around his chest eased somewhat, "but I'm glad to hear that."

"So, it really was an accident?" Samson asked carefully.

An odd look came over Elijah's face, as he shrugged. "As far as I know, yes."

"But you're not sure, are you?" Samson asked, sensing the hesitancy, pressing home the advantage of seeing that sudden change in his expression. "You're afraid that you weren't there and that somebody locked the door or deliberately stopped Scott from being able to open it."

Chef looked at him, then away instantly. "Don't know anything about it."

"Right, so we have another murder to add to somebody's damn checklist," Mountain muttered. "Amelia saw several people out there."

Elijah winced. "I wouldn't be passing around that information," he suggested, shaking his head.

"Meaning that the wrong person might hear about it? If that is so, you're right, and we're doing our best to keep her safe. She's also very vulnerable right now, medically fragile. Fending off yet another attack is not something we want her to deal with, not after all she's done and the injuries she's already sustained."

Elijah seemed to get a little agitated at that. But, as they waited, he calmed down, as if realizing they were biding their time and waiting for him to say something. He had no intention of doing that, but definitely something was there to tell.

Mountain stood up in frustration and looked over at Samson. "This is going nowhere. I'll come back later." Mountain stepped out, trying to figure out what to do next. Soon a text came through from one of the researchers, supplying them with information.

Elijah Williamson aka Chef had a son who was killed quite a few years ago. Military corps, a rescue gone

wrong. Your colonel there tried to save Chef's son. The colonel tried to get Chef's son out of the way and apparently did everything he could to keep him alive and out of the danger zone. Unfortunately Elijah's son was killed anyway.

With that information in his hand, he stepped back in, interrupting once again. Samson took one look at him and waited. Elijah glared at him cautiously, as if watching out for a viper. "The colonel tried to save your son, didn't he?"

He nodded slowly. "He did, yes, but it wasn't to be. He had him sent to a safer area, but then he was killed anyway," Chef confirmed.

"Okay, so that's partly why you have such a strong bond of loyalty with the colonel."

He nodded. "He's been there for me the entire time. He's a good man."

Mountain didn't say anything for a few moments. "Might be a good man but he's on his way out of the military, if the brass have any say in it." But Mountain was privy to a bit of information that not everybody knew. He looked over at Samson, who frowned at his notebook. "And I guess you've followed the colonel or requested to be on a lot of his posts too, haven't you?"

"Yeah, I have," Elijah admitted, with a mock smile. "Is that something that I'll be charged for too?" He was suddenly wary of the whole thing.

"No, not at all," Mountain said. "Has he come in to see you lately?"

"No, not a second time. Just once, when I was first brought here."

"I'm sorry. Sometimes things like this set people off."

He gave him a ghost of a smile. "And so they should. I wouldn't think any less of him because of that." And, with that, he shifted and spoke in a harsh tone. "Now, if you guys don't mind, I'm getting a little tired. and I'm done answering your questions."

Samson stood up. "That's fine. I'll come back and talk to you tomorrow."

He walked out with Mountain, who stood for a long moment, looking at Chef, trying to figure out what the hell was going on, why he wouldn't talk, what was holding him back. When Samson cleared his throat, Mountain nodded in agreement. "I'll talk to you later," he told Elijah, then quickly walked out.

In the hallway, he looked at Samson and asked in a whisper, "Did you get anything out of that?"

"I did get something out of that," Samson noted, "but I need to check a few details first."

"Can I get that information you just wrote up?"

"Yeah, I'll forward it to you," Samson said. "It should be in your email, but this text will get it to you a little faster." He looked up at the *ding.* "There it is."

Mountain watched him carefully, asking, "Have you talked to Ted at all?"

"I talk to him all the time," Samson replied, turning back to look at him. "Why?"

"Wondering how he's holding up."

"He's holding, not great, especially after what happened to Jerry, but I think this case is taking a toll on him."

"It's taking a toll on everybody," Mountain replied, his voice harsh. "And that won't change."

"No, it won't. Not until we solve it," Samson noted. "I don't know about you, but I'm starting to feel very much as if we're on the cusp of that."

And, with that surprising announcement, Samson turned and walked away, leaving Mountain staring at him.

AMELIA LOOKED OVER at Sydney and suggested in a light tone. "You could lock me in for tonight, and I should be fine, right?"

Sydney nodded. "You're *probably* fine," she clarified, "but I can't make that decision. Security is up to the men to decide on."

Amelia groaned. "Seriously, I still have to be under their watch?"

"Absolutely," Sydney declared, yet with a cheerful smile. "And, to top it all off, you're supposed to be grateful."

Amelia snickered. "Oh, I am. I'm grateful that I'm alive, and I'm grateful for your medical intervention that's kept me that way. However, I could just as easily go to the village now. They could take care of me just fine."

"If the guys thought that you could protect yourself, then I am certain they would release you," Sydney replied, "but I'm not getting the impression that they're feeling very positive in that direction."

Amelia groaned. "No, I'm not either, unfortunately, yet I really would appreciate an end to all this cloak-and-dagger stuff."

"Talk to them about that," Sydney suggested. "I'm sure Mountain will be back soon."

"He seems to be one of the worst to listen to my requests," she muttered, with half a smile.

"Worst or best, depending on the way you want to look at it," Sydney pointed out. "Remember. These guys have gone to a lot of effort to try and sort this mess out, on the base and in regard to your shootings in particular. Still, I know it doesn't look as if it's happening very quickly or easily, but I think they're probably getting pretty damn close now."

"Do you think so?"

Just then the door to the clinic opened, and, sure enough, Mountain walked in. He looked over at Amelia and smiled. "Seems the ladies are getting restless."

Amelia nodded. "Kind of. I was thinking that you guys could let me go to the village, and I could stay there."

"I don't think that's a good idea," he stated immediately.

She frowned, and he frowned right back. "Why is that?" she asked, hating the bitterness in her question that revealed her state of mind.

"Because I don't want you taking anything dangerous to them."

That shut her up immediately, not what she had expected. She stared at him in mute frustration. "So, you think somebody will come after me?"

"I don't know, but I don't want to take the chance, do you?"

She glared at him. "That's a low blow, and you know I don't want to."

"Then stay and let us handle this. And you're not that much better, no matter how much you keep trying to convince Sydney that you are."

Sydney burst out laughing. "Don't drag me into this, Mountain. I know exactly how she's doing, thank you very much. She is certainly doing better, but she's definitely not ready to be moving around, much less heading outside and taking on the world. If we could safely get her up and mobile again, I would be happy, but I'm not sure that she's ready for that stage either."

"I'm obviously in the way, causing trouble, and taking up valuable manpower," Amelia explained. "So, it makes more sense for me to go back to the village, where I know that my people would look after me."

"Sure, but tell me this," Mountain began. "Do you absolutely, … 100 percent, know that nobody in or around that village is a part of this?"

"What do you mean by a *part* of it?" she asked.

"Such as, did they take money to help out Eric or his partners-in-crime in terrorizing the base?" he asked bluntly. "Did any of the villagers accept a bribe in lieu of helping somebody at this base who died here?" As she stared at him, he continued. "Did they buy equipment or accept equipment, money, cash, food, favors, future favors, or anything else instead of or in lieu of helping out missing persons before they died from hypothermia? Every time I went to the village to get answers, they all closed rank on me. Not a one gave me any useful information." She sat back and stared at him, and he nodded. "See? It's more complicated than you think. So, if you can't promise me that, absolutely no way can I guarantee you'll be safe there. And, if I can't guarantee your safety, no way you're leaving."

She glared at him. "So, now you're making my friends and family out to be serial killers?"

"No, I'm really not, but I also don't want anything else to happen to you." Her mouth opened at that, then she snapped it shut. When she glared at him, he gave her a big grin. "See? You don't even have an answer for me."

"It's hard to have answers when you say those things," she muttered.

"Why?" He kept it up, intentionally pushing her a bit. "You know perfectly well that we've done a lot to keep you alive, and we'll continue to do more. Obviously we want to do everything we can, but *we* won't take any risks with you. Now if you intend to take risks yourself, it's better you rethink that because that means you're not yet of sound mind and judgment."

She snorted at that. "I think you're making up this shit," she muttered, staring at him.

He burst out laughing. "You could be right, but can you really take that chance with your own life?"

"No, of course I can't," she replied, raising both her hands in frustration. "Even the thought of taking any of this craziness over to my people … is unacceptable."

"Exactly, so you need to give us a chance and to take this time to regain some of your strength," Mountain stated, patting her on the shoulder. "If somebody were to come in and attack you—assuming they'd taken out whatever guard we had stationed in the hallway—you're not even close to being capable of defending yourself. So, until that state is reached, no way you're leaving. Not on my watch."

He turned and walked to the door, where he smiled at Sydney. "Don't forget to get dinner, Sydney," he reminded her in a cheerful tone. "I'll go grab a plate. Then I'll come back and stand guard." And, with that, he was gone.

Amelia let out her breath slowly, followed by an irate half-muted scream of rage.

Sydney looked over at her and smiled. "Mountain doesn't want anything to happen to you, but, if you listen carefully, an awful lot of caring is in the back of his tone as he says it."

"What?" She stared at Sydney in astonishment.

"Mountain doesn't let very much out at any point in time, particularly his innermost feelings. The fact that he's even saying what he has so far tells me an awful lot about how he's feeling." And, with that, Sydney smiled, walked closer to the door. "Now, why don't you think about that for a few minutes? As soon as he gets back, I'll go collect some food. In the meantime, I'll step out into the hallway and make a couple phone calls."

After Sydney exited the clinic, it wasn't long before Amelia heard the doc's voice on the phone. Sydney only did that when she was trying to have private conversations—understandably so since she was a doctor and her patients were entitled to confidentiality, even in these close quarters.

Amelia immediately reconsidered what Sydney had suggested about Mountain caring more than his words let on. The whole idea of that didn't even make sense to Amelia, since, in her mind, the man didn't know her at all, didn't seemed interested in her in that way.

What's more, at the rate they were going with this investigation, there wouldn't be anything nice about her to know. She sagged into the hospital bed, frustrated and hating the intense fatigue and weakness that overtook her after a confrontation. She didn't do confrontations well, and the thought of trying to fight for her freedom had already gotten her up in arms before he'd even arrived. And now it seemed as if he could win without her having the strength to fight, and that frustrated her all the more.

She didn't like being weak and hated the thought of being perceived as weak by others, even though Mountain would immediately deny viewing her that way. Still, in her current physical state, it was hard not to feel weak. If she were in a losing battle of some kind, she wouldn't like it. It was a good ten minutes before the door opened again, and, expecting it to be Sydney, Amelia was surprised when Mountain walked in.

He had a plate heaped full of food. The minute she looked at it, her stomach started to rumble. He nodded. "You're hungry. That's good, right? I can hear it clear over here." She must have been giving off some cantankerous vibes because he shook his head. "Come on. Time for sharing a good meal among friends, not fighting," he muttered.

"Yeah, well, if I had some good friends here, I might consider that. In the meantime, I don't have that option, so touché."

He nodded, then shrugged and didn't say anything.

She glared at him. "Are you always like this?"

"No, not always, but I really do work at it."

Such honesty filled his tone that she almost cracked up laughing. "Really?" she asked in a dry voice. "And here I thought being irritating came to you naturally."

"Oh, no, I have to work at it really hard. Just ask Teegan."

She rolled her eyes at that. "I would love to, but nobody's allowed me to talk to Teegan yet. Remember?" Her tone had a definite bite to it.

He eyed her and nodded. "That's a good point. Do you want to talk to him after dinner?"

"Yes, of course," she said immediately.

He pulled out his phone and apparently sent his brother a text message. "He'll come by after dinner," Mountain stated, reading Teegan's response.

"Fine." Amelia sighed, as she sagged back. "I haven't had any food yet either."

"And you will get some very soon. Sydney's gone to get it. I would offer you some of this, but Sydney is very particular about what she thinks will be the best for you. I found that out the hard way, while Teegan was in that very bed for quite a stint himself."

She looked ruefully at his heavily laden plate. "Which likely means something light, maybe soup or broth."

"Do you think you can handle much more than that?"

She contemplated it and then shook her head. "Probably not." She groaned. "Every time I think I'm doing better, something happens, and I'm doing worse."

"I don't think you're doing worse at all," he countered. "I think you're impatient, and that's always the dangerous time."

"Why is that?" she asked, knowing that she wouldn't like the answer.

"Because people tend to expect more out of themselves, and they do way more than they should because they think they're on the mend or should be. What ends up happening is that they overdo it completely and set themselves back … or worse."

"You think so?"

"I know so. I've seen it countless times, and, hell, I've done it myself. In your case, as low as your blood count was, you still can't risk any bleeding. That's why you feel so weak with any exertion at all. This time is an opportunity for you to sit back and relax. This is your chance to heal, and we want to make sure that you heal 100 percent, so you can come back to this frozen land that you love so much."

She settled back down on her bed, studying him, stunned at the passion in his voice. "You love it up here too, don't you?" she asked him.

"I've always loved the Arctic and being up here," he murmured, "but, then again, I also love a nice warm sandy beach," he added, with a big grin. "There's room for all of it, you know?"

"There is, but it's just been a whole lot easier for me to find acceptance up here."

"Because there's not all that much competition, I presume."

"Meaning, I wouldn't hold my own if there were?" she asked a little testily.

"God, no. Meaning that you wouldn't feel you always have to be on guard," he clarified. "Do you think I don't see that? I don't know whether it's all because of your heritage and the bias you've encountered, or it's all about that one guy you dated and you have become wary of all men."

"Wary of all men," she noted in a wry tone. "At least that's how I would interpret it," she murmured, seeing the shadow that crossed his face. "I'm sure some of your psychologists would come up with a million other things in addition to that."

"Doesn't matter whether they would or not," he replied on a laugh. "It's all about you and who you are, not about them at all." Once again he'd completely surprised her, and she didn't know what to say. He looked at her and laughed and asked, "Cat got your tongue, did it?"

"You keep surprising me."

"Not meaning to," he replied, with a shrug. "I'm just being me."

"Being you is a gift though," she admitted, "and it's not

one that I'm used to."

"And that's the problem," he pointed out. "You're expecting trouble, and there isn't any, at least as far as I'm concerned. As long as I can keep you safe, I'm content. The minute I have to fight you over that, we've got a problem."

She snorted. "So, what you're saying is, as long as I do what you tell me to do, we're fine, but the minute I don't, then we've got a problem."

He flashed her a bright grin and nodded. "Yeah, that works."

"It doesn't work for me," she snapped, "particularly not long-term."

"I didn't say anything about long-term. I'm talking about while we get you back on your feet. It's not any workable solution on a long-term basis. Besides, who wants a relationship with a dishrag?" Her jaw dropped at that, and he burst out laughing. "I know. I know. We aren't there yet."

"You've got to be kidding me."

"I understand. I absolutely surprised myself when I first figured it out. It's definitely not where I thought I would be heading, but it's hard to miss the connection."

"It's totally easy to miss the connection," she argued. "I already missed it myself."

At that, he burst out laughing. "You might be wishing that you missed it," he replied, giving her a knowing look that made her blush, "but it's perfectly obvious what's going on between us to anybody willing to look."

She sagged back on her bed, shaking her head. "I would have to be suicidal."

"No," he argued, "but you will certainly need to be your own person because I could never be with somebody who can't be real."

"I don't think I can get much more real," she muttered, "and you've already seen all the ugly bits."

"I've also seen all the beautiful bits too," he noted, with a big grin.

At that, she flushed a bright red and glared at him.

"Hey, we were trying to save your life at the time, and I really did try not to look."

"Right," she muttered, with an eye roll. "That would be so you."

"Hey," he said, with an almost injured air. "I pride myself on being an honorable man."

"Yeah, right," she replied, with a frown. "That doesn't mean you didn't look while you had the chance."

"Honestly I was too busy trying to help Sydney staunch the bleeding that you were busy spewing out all over the floor, which was enough to drop me at any moment," he pointed out. "Saving your life was the first priority. Keeping you warm was the second. You weren't giving us any help on either issue," he stated, "and that made our lives very difficult."

She pondered that. "I guess I was in pretty rough shape, wasn't I?"

"Pretty rough shape? No. Hell no. Not even close to that. You were two steps from death, and, if it wasn't for Sydney being right here, I don't know what medical care you would have gotten. She's brilliant, and she's kept everybody alive who could be kept alive. So, I certainly don't begrudge her any minutes of spare time or supplies to do the job that she's doing."

"That's really nice of you," she admitted, surprised that he would even say that.

"This is a military clinic, not some fancy private hospital.

Some of the brass always worries about costs," he acknowledged. "Sometimes with justification, sometimes not," he muttered. "Yet people still look at the budget and groan and complain. In your case, whatever it took, we were happy to try it."

"I would be happy to think that you would help anybody to the maximum extent possible," she murmured. "Not just me. Although I understand from your perspective the sense of urgency was higher, in case I knew anything as to what all was going on."

He gave her a grave nod. "We would have helped anybody as much as we could, of course, yet you're right. It was more of an issue for me personally because I needed to find out what was going on with my brother."

"But you've had him for some time now."

"Yes, we have him back safe and sound, and we owe you for that. However, we didn't know whether you'd had anything to do with his original kidnapping." She gasped, her eyes opening wide to stare at him, her jaw dropping. He nodded. "When you look at it from our perspective, we didn't know who and what had created this issue in the first place."

"Good Lord, is that why I'm under guard?" She spoke in a hushed tone, as her face ran through a series of multiple colors. "I … Am I a prisoner here?" she asked, shifting in the bed in outrage, trying to sort out the information that came through. Panic warred with fear that anybody could think such a thing.

"No. I certainly don't think you had anything to do with it, but obviously there are questions."

"Of course there are questions," she muttered, as she sagged back slowly, wincing with pain as she finally managed to relax enough to look at him. "Let me talk to your brother, stat."

"I know he really wants to talk to you, but I've been holding off. He'll be here in a little while."

"Why not call him right now? Or is it because you don't trust me?" she asked bitterly.

"No, not at all. Honestly, I've been holding off because I didn't want to trigger a relapse in either one of you."

"What? Is he okay?" she asked immediately, her anger swept away by concern.

"He's doing better every day, but he doesn't have any answers either. And he's still not 100 percent."

"How can that be?"

"His recovery is going well, at least where his body is concerned, but he's had a great deal of memory loss, which we've attributed to drugs involved in his capture, though we lack information on that."

She winced. "Yes, I tried to keep him stable, plus tried to get information out of him myself. He kept telling me that I couldn't take him back and couldn't take him to the village, so I had to look after him and keep him alive on my own. In fact, … whatever information he had was important," she added, suddenly frowning. "You need to get that out of him in some way."

"You didn't say anything about that before, about the information he had."

"I didn't remember anything about it," she replied, "until now." She groaned, as she collapsed back again. "Hell, for all I know, I did have something to do with his kidnapping."

He got up, walked a few steps closer, and looked down at her. "Look," he said in a soothing voice. "I know you didn't have anything to do with it, and I can understand the frustration of not getting the information you need out of your brain right now. Maybe something is in there to get, or maybe not. The thing is, we won't know until we know, and there will be time soon enough for that."

"I don't know what to think anymore," she muttered. "Please let me talk to him."

He hesitated, then nodded. "I'll go get him. I need to post another guard on the door first." And, with that, he walked out of the room.

She expected him to come back immediately, but it was a good twenty minutes before the clinic door opened, and Mountain made his way back to her. The minute she saw Teegan, tears filled her eyes. She opened her arms, and he walked over and gave her a big hug, tears in his eyes as well.

"My brother has been keeping you all to himself," Teegan noted, with a big cheeky grin, as he sat near her. "I think he's jealous of our relationship."

She snorted at that. "No, he's trying to keep me isolated, you know, prisoner tactics, trying to find out what I know." She had caught on to that, even if it wasn't his intent.

At that, Teegan winced and replied, "Unfortunately, knowing him, … I think that is quite possible."

"Oh, please," Mountain said testily from the doorway. He had crossed his arms, watching them closely. "You two can bond over whatever the hell you want," he muttered, "but I need to hear every word you say because neither one of you has the answers we need, and I'm hoping that, maybe together, … between the two of you, we can stir up those muddy memories."

"And yet you held off letting me come in here," Teegan noted, glaring at his brother.

"Yeah, and, if you take a good look, … you'll realize

she's not going anywhere very soon. Look at her. The minute I see her energy drop or anything that looks suspicious about her condition, you'll get your ass kicked out of here too."

Teegan nodded. "That's fair," he admitted, as he turned to look at Amelia. "I am really glad to see you," he said, as Mountain took up a seat at the end of the hospital bed, his arms still crossed as he glared at the two of them.

She wasn't sure what was making him angry. Plus, she's the one who should have been mad. Still, even as she thought about everything that had happened, she realized she lacked the energy to even consider it. "I didn't have anything to do with Teegan's kidnapping," she muttered.

"Mountain knows that," Teegan stated, looking at her in surprise. His gaze traveled to his brother, and he glared at the expression on his face. "I told you that she didn't."

"Yet you also can't tell me who did. So, until that point gets resolved, we need to ensure that nobody gets a free pass. Not even Amelia."

"I forgot what a hard-ass you could be," Teegan muttered.

"You shouldn't have," Mountain snapped, brutally dark. "You know perfectly well what I'm doing is protocol, and we can't unmake the rules just because we want to."

Teegan winced. "I know, and next you'll tell me that, if I wasn't so emotional, we wouldn't be having this conversation."

"That's quite right as well, isn't it? You are losing sight of the problems here, thinking with your—"

"I'm thinking with my heart," Teegan admitted, cutting him off, and that earned him a hard stare. "This woman saved me, and I know perfectly well she had absolutely nothing to do with everything going wrong in my world. I

know I had some vital information, but, whatever it was, …
I can't remember it. So apparently it's still not enough to do
us any good."

"And yet it's something," Mountain said. "Keep in mind
that we still have information coming in constantly. Right
now, we have information coming in every ten minutes …
literally." As his phone buzzed, he pulled it out, looked at it,
frowned, and tucked it away.

Teegan frowned at him too and pointed to his phone.
"Like that?"

"Yeah, just like that. I'm trying to let it all jell in my
brain before I do something about it because I still don't
have the proof that we need. I need to make this stick."

"Do you know who did it?" Teegan asked, as he jumped
to his feet and walked over to glare at his big brother.
Mountain remained silent. "You're not sharing?" Teegan
asked.

"No, I'm not sharing," he stated, staring at Teegan with
the same indomitable look he'd used when Teegan was
growing up. "No way I'm letting you go off half-cocked."

"I wouldn't go off half-cocked," he declared, glaring at
his brother. "I'm not a kid anymore, and you'll have to let
me grow up some day."

Mountain's eyebrows shot up. "Presumably on a day
when you don't find yourself kidnapped and lost out in the
middle of the Arctic, *huh*?"

At that, Teegan rolled his eyes. "You can't upset me because I know everything you do and say is really based in
love, despite how it may sound. Thus it's pretty hard to
argue with you," he muttered, as he turned back toward
Amelia. "He really is a good guy."

Amelia nodded. "I don't have a problem with that. And

since I don't have as many answers as I would like either, I can't really argue with him. In that, at least, he is right."

"And yet you did argue with me," Mountain added in a casual voice. "Still, you've given us a lot more information on various people than we had."

"Really?" Teegan turned to look at her. "Did you see what happened?"

She shook her head immediately. "No, I didn't, not with you, but I'd seen things out there before, and I'd watched you guys from a distance quite a bit. I couldn't really identify who anybody was, but still …"

"Right." Teegan nodded. "From a distance it's hard, isn't it?"

"And yet mannerisms and movements, posture and the way people walk, are all quite literally identifiable," Mountain agreed, as he turned to Teegan. "She saw somebody line up a shot intended for Elijah."

Teegan stared at his brother for a long moment, then turned to look back at Amelia. "I think in that case, you probably did make a mistake," he murmured softly. "Elijah doesn't go out."

"It was him," she declared. "I have seen him out, not on a regular basis—there you are correct—but he did go out occasionally, and I can say that with certainly. A couple times, on rare occasions, I've even seen your colonel out there."

"You did? Seriously?" Mountain asked.

"Yes. Not as often, but then it's hit and miss, who I see and when I see them," she shared, looking from one to the other. "It's not as if I was sitting around and doing nothing but stalking your military base. That is not the impression I want you to get because nothing could be further from the truth. I was out there working my ass off, trying to collect my own scientific data, so that I had something to work with, once I got back home again. So, it was important for me to not only keep Teegan alive but to keep my own work functioning and alive as well," she said bitterly.

"I've spent a lifetime on this work, and I wasn't about to let it all go because of whatever mess you guys had going on. But I couldn't leave Teegan for long, and that caused some complications. I had to make a lot of trips, risk being seen, and burn through a lot of extra calories. Often Elijah gave me extra supplies to make it through."

"Did you have any association with Elijah prior to this particular survival session?" Mountain asked. "Did you know him well from before? Do you have any personal relationship with him?"

She looked at him in surprise, then shook her head. "I've seen him in prior training sessions, but I didn't interact with him much before. However, he obviously has a heart for people, and he was just trying to help. He may well have been doing it outside his authority, and, for that, I probably owe your program some extra funding to cover the costs, but honestly it wasn't very much. It was leftovers, pantry goods, and bandages and stuff."

Mountain nodded. "Nobody will begrudge you or anybody else a meal or medical supplies out there," he replied in a casual tone. "The problems come when it's more than that in terms of supplies, such as weapons."

"No, nothing like that was given to me," she stated, with a wave of her hand. "I'm certainly capable of hunting anything I need to hunt. And I have weapons stashed out there that I doubt any of you guys would ever find." Mountain stiffened and looked at her in shock. She nodded. "It's suicidal to be out there without some form of self-defense," she pointed out, looking at him, "as you well know. Absolutely no way you would travel here without something to keep you safe."

"I get that."

"And, before you ask, my weapons are all licensed, and they're all registered," she added.

"Yet they didn't come up in any search of you," he noted, looking at her.

"Depends on what database you used," she said. "Essentially I come from a Canadian background, and I hold dual citizenship. The weapons are registered in Canada because I use them up here, and I don't travel with them across borders."

"Right." He frowned. "Would anybody else have known about them?"

"Only if they saw me hunting," she replied. "I only hunted when I had to, and it's not my choice to kill animals unless it's for my self-preservation or involves a predator or something like that. And, no, I haven't had to shoot any predators or defend myself this year. In the past I have, but not this year," she muttered. "But, yes, I hunt and can certainly hunt enough to keep me—and Teegan—alive. However, when things got a little scarce, and I was burning the candle at both ends, I wouldn't say no to a few extra supplies, especially when I was trying to help Teegan."

"Right," Mountain agreed. "Again, we won't worry about a few groceries that you used from here, while trying to keep somebody alive from this base." He snorted. "That would be ludicrous."

"All of it's ludicrous," Teegan stated. "We already help the village and the science camp as it is."

"And the village helped me," she added, "at least a couple times. I would come and go with no regular patterns, so nobody could track me. I always made sure I was somewhere between here and there, in case I ran into trouble, so I would have somebody nearby if I needed help. Plus I have access to my own science camp, but I had to keep these trips hidden."

"That's smart."

"I hope so. I kept an ear to the ground and paid a few people for information," she admitted, and Mountain rolled his eyes at that. "I needed intel, in order to keep an eye on whether anybody was hunting us or was out looking. Obviously I knew about you, and of course I saw you, but I didn't know what your relationship was with Teegan, so I didn't know if you were friend or foe."

Mountain nodded. "Once we found Terrence alive, after he had gone missing, I had more hope in my heart that we would find Teegan. Even finding Yegorahn's body gave me hope, since obviously someone else was involved in prolonging his life. I guess I always knew Teegan was alive, and I figured something had to be going on—either he was seriously injured or he was being held against his will. It never occurred to me that somebody was helping him to stay alive, keeping him hidden because they were afraid for his life. So, thank you for that."

"I'm glad to hear that," Amelia said, "because sometimes you seem to blame me."

"No, I don't blame you at all," Mountain clarified immediately. "How could I when you saved Teegan's life? But this whole thing is a major shit show, and, while I have a pretty good idea who is behind it all, getting the proof I need is a problem, and I'll definitely need proof … because I doubt this person will volunteer anything."

"Set a trap," Teegan suggested.

Mountain shook his head. "He's too wily and has been doing this too long for that. However, some shift is happening right now, and I'm trying to make use of it, though I'm not quite sure how to do it yet," he admitted, turning to look at his brother. "I really don't need interference at the moment."

"Maybe not," Teegan replied, "but surely you could use a hand."

"That's why I also have quite a few guys up here who will help."

At that, Teegan frowned. "What's the deal with that new investigator?" he asked, with a searching gaze. "Something's familiar yet odd about him."

"Have you worked with him before?" Mountain asked, his eyebrows going up.

"I don't think so, but … things are still on the hazy side."

"I certainly don't have any reason to doubt that he's a good guy," Mountain began, "so I'm totally okay with keeping him in the loop."

"Still taking a chance though, aren't you?" Teegan asked, frowning at him. "That seems odd for you."

"So you say," he quipped, with a twinkle in his gaze. "You'll find out the truth about that soon enough."

"If you say so." Teegan shrugged. Then he yawned.

Amelia immediately took his hand. "You need to go lie down."

Mountain rolled his eyes at her.

However, Teegan didn't. "Now that voice is something I remember very clearly."

"What voice?" she asked.

"Yours, saying I'm in trouble, that I needed more rest. The same voice telling me to eat and to take medicine. The same voice telling me to hang on, to be still, to sleep. It's almost as if it's burned into my brain."

"Part of it is," she said, with a chuckle. "I worked hard at burning all that into your brain," she muttered. "It's hardly wasted though."

"Maybe not, but holy—"

She laughed, and then coughed, wincing, as her body shuddered with pain.

Immediately Teegan stood, studying her. "I'll let you rest. I'll be back after I have a nap too," he said, as he rolled his eyes at her, "if only to keep you and my big brother happy. Then I'll pick up some dinner. Speaking of which, how about I bring you back something light and easy to eat, like soup?"

"That would be lovely," she replied. "I think Sydney went to get me something, but it seems she's been held up. In the meantime, I guess I'll have a nap myself."

"Sounds good," he murmured, as he looked over at Mountain intently, "unless big brother here has a problem with it."

Immediately Mountain shook his head. "No, I don't. Besides, any extra help to keep her safe will never be wrong at this point."

Teegan nodded at him, and, as they both looked back at her, she motioned with her hand to the door. "Go," she told Teegan. "I'll have a nap and talk to you guys later." She closed her eyes and quickly fell asleep.

THE SPEED WITH which Amelia fell asleep was pretty amazing. Mountain tiptoed out of the room, as Sydney walked back in with a tray, took one look at Amelia, and smiled. "She's done really well, but her body needs rest."

Teegan looked back at her, worried. "She might have done really well, but she still seems to be quite exhausted. She went to such lengths to keep me alive. I sure don't want anything to happen to her."

"And nothing will," Sydney declared, with a cheerful smile. "As long as you guys make sure whoever did this to her doesn't get a chance at her again. That'll be the challenge we'll have from here on in."

Mountain nodded. "That's exactly why everybody is on guard duty. I need to put an end to this and damn fast." At that, Sydney and Teegan both turned and stared at him. He nodded. "I do know who," he admitted. "I don't know how and why."

"You can always call on us to help, you know?" Teegan offered.

"I know, but here's the thing. I need to get this to stop permanently, with an actual conviction and not just a pass up the hierarchy," Mountain explained, "and that'll be a whole different story."

"The military does have a problem with that, doesn't it?" Sydney asked.

"Too often when there's a problem, they move people up and down," Mountain noted. "They'll move someone up because there's no proof, and that takes them from the situation without a fuss, but that won't help us." He shook his head. "This is bigger than that. It's too damn big, and it's got to stop."

"Do you think it goes back to Nikolai's father?" Teegan

asked.

"Oh, that's part of it," he confirmed, as he stared down at the sleeping woman. He shook his head and then stopped himself from saying anything else. He closed his mouth and let it go, since they didn't need to worry about the trouble this was bound to bring. "I'll see you guys in a bit." And, with that, he turned and headed down to the hallway.

His brother came after him and called out. "You don't have to do everything alone, you know?"

He smiled and looked back at him. "No, but sometimes I really do. There's a hell of a lot of difference between your position right now and mine," he pointed out, then shrugged. "While I'm okay to lose everything I've gained, you're still at the point of needing all this."

"That's not helping …"

Mountain held up a hand to stop him. "Look. If I get fired, that's fine. I'll walk away and be happy about it, now that I know you're safe," he shared, giving his brother a wry look. "Believe me, searching for you all these weeks has completely changed my attitude about where I want my life going in the future."

Teegan reached out and gripped his brother's shoulder. "You and me both. Nothing like lying there dying, knowing you're one step away from never seeing the family you care about so much. I prayed so damn hard for you to show up," Teegan admitted, with a sigh. "Of course when you do, you bring all kinds of chaos along with you."

Mountain roared with laughter. "I don't know about my bringing chaos. It seems to me that was your department this time, and you left a trail of it in your wake."

And, with that, he left Teegan at his room and headed to meet Samson. Mountain knocked on the doorframe, then poked his head in to find Samson waiting for him.

"How is she?" Samson asked.

"She's good, bits and pieces are coming, a little at a time it seems." Mountain relayed what she'd remembered this time.

Samson nodded. "All of it fits, but what we don't have is anything to brace him about, and, if we go to the brass, nobody'll believe us."

"I know it."

"I've been sitting here thinking about it, and I think Chef will be our best bet to breaking things wide open."

"And yet that loyalty, if that's what it is happening, is deadly strong."

"It is, and I've been doing some research into his background," Samson shared, "so listen to this." And he quickly relayed how the colonel had moved Chef's son to another base, so that he would be safer.

Mountain nodded. "I heard that from Elijah directly."

"Yeah, that's what you heard," Samson clarified, "but then I found another file. This file was buried a little deeper, and I'm sure not too many people even know about it." And he proceeded to read off information that had Mountain staring at him in shock.

"Well, shit," Mountain muttered.

"That's one word for it, all right."

"So, how do we use this information to open up Elijah Williamson," Mountain asked. "If you ask me, it seems to be a pretty underhanded trick."

"I don't know about that," Samson countered, "but something is definitely here."

"I was also wondering if some other person is involved, someone who has some hold on Elijah because what else would bring about this kind of loyalty?"

"And yet he's of an age that, in many ways, … I'm not sure he would care," Samson said, continuing to explore and dissect their interrogation and Mason's intel.

"Maybe not, but I'm not sure I'm convinced."

"No, I'm definitely not either," Samson agreed. "I've asked for more information on this second Elijah file because I don't have anything official on it. It's just a footnote in the original Elijah file that I have here."

"And those footnotes have a habit of disappearing, if we're not careful," Mountain warned.

"They do, indeed," Samson noted.

"That's one of the reasons why I have somebody outside looking in," Mountain muttered.

"That would help, as long as it won't get their ass kicked too." Samson laughed.

"Ass-kicking is pretty well part of their business."

"Anyway, in our consideration of all this, we must be prepared that, if we can't find any proof, anything positive, that this is likely to end up being a full wash."

"We can't let that happen," Mountain declared.

"We don't even know how long this has gone on."

"Which is one of the reasons why I requested more information," Mountain stated calmly. "As far as I'm concerned, the more information we have, the better off we are going forward; but it won't be that easy because some of this stuff's been buried for a long time."

Then Samson's phone buzzed, and he checked it and nodded. "This is an interesting note," he said, as he held up his phone for Mountain to read.

He studied the message and shook his head. "Jesus," he swore, "if they have that in writing, something in a file, it's just that much more ammo."

"It is, indeed," Samson confirmed. "Have you checked on Elijah recently?"

"No, I haven't," Mountain said, immediately getting to his feet. "It was on my mind to do so, and then I ended up back over with Amelia."

Samson gave him a crooked grin. "Finding it easy to get sidetracked with her around, are you?"

"Yeah, and that's shitty too because there shouldn't be any *getting sidetracked* with all this crap to deal with."

"Hey, go easy on yourself. The impression I got is that you've not considered anybody a viable option in terms of your personal world for a very long time."

"If ever," he added, with a wry look at Samson. "But I'm really not into dissecting my personal relationships just now either."

Samson burst out laughing and nodded. "No, I can see that would be a bit of a challenge, quite a challenge. Anyway I'll start collating this, while you go check on Elijah and see what his mood is like. Try not to poke him too much because we'll have a big battle coming. ... Maybe see how much loyalty there is. Once you involve your kids, everything changes."

"As you should know," Mountain said, with a cheeky grin.

Samson laughed. "Absolutely."

And, with that, Mountain headed down to see how Chef was doing. As he walked in, he saw the big man crashed on the floor, silent and still, as if prepared to be here forever. Mountain walked over and sat down beside Chef with a *thud.* "Man, I sure wish you would release the burden from your soul."

Elijah looked up at him and replied, "That goes for you too. With the line of work that we're in, there is no releasing of burdens, but you already know that. So, why are you asking me to? You have just as many demons in your world."

"God, I hope not," Mountain said, with a mock laugh. "I have a lot, and some of them will never go away, and I know that, but the thought of having this forever? Well, that's a little harsh."

"And yet you know as well as I do that it is what it is."

"It is, and yet …" He gave Chef a pointed look and let it hang there. "If you're the one who takes the fall, that's one thing, but to let the other person involved in this go free, to continue as is?" He shook his head. "That's a completely different story."

It had been a shot in the dark, but, as soon as Chef's face shifted and darkened, Mountain realized that the shot in the dark had hit a target. He nodded, giving him a feral grin. "Yeah, we know. We know all kinds of things. And believe me, it's not making anybody happy, but knowing is a far cry from proving something."

"And if you can't prove it, you don't need to even go in that direction," Elijah snapped, "because there's no joy for anybody."

"Except you," Mountain countered, with a wry look. "You get to be loyal to the very end, right?"

"I *am* loyal to the end," he stated.

"What if it's misplaced? What if that loyalty is something that shouldn't have even happened?"

Elijah frowned, clearly confused. "No way that's possible. Believe me. … I spent a lifetime doing this," he muttered.

"But what if your son had not died?" Mountain asked.

"I would happily have spent my lifetime with my son, but I didn't get that option," he added, his voice harsh.

"I'm surprised you stayed in the military after that."

"I didn't have anywhere else to go," Chef admitted. "My wife passed away. My son was gone. So what was I to do? At least here … I had a home. I had a family of sorts. Even though some of their orders seemed like death wishes sometimes," he shared, with an eye roll, "I didn't particularly care. I was doing what I could to make people happy on a regular basis, and that's all that mattered. Now, if you don't mind, I want a nap." And, with that, he gave Mountain a bland smile and waved at the door, "Go on. Get lost. You've got better things to do than torment me."

"And what if I do have better things to do? Very productive things."

"If you had them, you wouldn't be here fishing," Chef stated calmly. "And the minute you do have them, I suspect everything will change." He smiled. "In the meantime, nothing's changing. It's all exactly as it always has been, and, at this point, I think it's all it'll ever be."

"And what happens when you're not there?" Mountain asked. "Have you considered that?"

"I have, and I don't have any solution." And, on that cryptic note, he stretched out and closed his eyes.

Mountain, knowing there was no point in talking to Chef's stubborn ass anymore, got up and headed out.

"Say hi to Amelia for me," Elijah told Mountain, as he walked out.

"I will. We're trying to keep her alive too." When no further reaction came from Elijah, Mountain added, "You can do your bit and help on that project too. I don't know why she has to die in this deal."

"She doesn't have to die," he declared, opening his eyes and frowning at Mountain. "Why does she have to die?"

"We would like to think that she doesn't, but, after two attempts on her life, we're not so sure that somebody's prepared to let her walk free," Mountain shared, feeling a fatigue that had been there since he'd arrived. The hope of finding Teegan alive was now a reality. However, with so many other elements at play, Mountain could still feel that same tiredness everywhere.

"You need to keep her safe then."

"It's hard, not knowing where the attack will come from. It's also hard knowing that somebody could help but won't."

And, with that parting shot delivered, Mountain turned and left Elijah to consider it all alone.

DAY 6 MORNING

AMELIA WOKE UP and yawned, feeling a more normal lassitude in her body that she hadn't felt in a while. Every time she had come here to the military base over the last three months or so, it had been a physical endurance test, mostly because she did it to herself, overdoing it out in the Arctic tundra, knowing that her time was running out and that she wouldn't get all the data that she wanted this time. It was all about making hay, while there was hay to make.

Now, however, winding up in the medical clinic at the military base was not how she'd expected this last trip of hers to end up. Yet she was grateful for the peace and the sense of recovery she felt. Anything that could make her life a little easier right now was a godsend, and she would take it quite happily.

She shifted gently and reached for the water at her side. Sydney sat at her desk as always, a reliable guardian angel, someone Amelia would have to thank in some special way when this was all over.

As if hearing her muted thoughts, Sydney looked up at her patient and smiled. "Hey. How are you feeling?"

"I feel decent," Amelia said, with half a smile, "although I'm not sure *decent* is quite the right word."

"No, but as long as you're on the mend, starting to improve, we'll take it," the doc replied, as she came over and picked up the blood pressure cuff. Quickly she did a quick round, checking Amelia's vitals and her wounds.

"Surely I'm getting better, and I don't need all that anymore."

"You'll always need that because it's one of tools that we have to confirm that your improvement is steadfast and solid," Sydney explained. "Honest to God, I don't ever want to see somebody else as close to death as you were and not have any blood to give them."

"Was it that bad?"

"It's one thing to be in a full medical facility, but, when I'm out here in the frozen tundra, it's not possible," she shared. "The triage decisions out here are the worst of the worst. It's like trying to make a decision whether you'll give CPR to somebody—when you're alone with your patient out in the middle of nowhere, and nobody can reach you or even knows to reach you within an hour or less. As medical professionals, we can't do CPR forever, and we must decide whether we'll even try." Sydney gave a sad smile. "Once you make those kinds of life-and-death decisions"—she shook her head—"everything else in the world becomes something you don't know any longer."

"That sounds terrible," Amelia muttered in agreement.

"It is, and it can be … hard. Life is precious and fills us with joy, and it's one of those things you should enjoy fully, if you get the opportunity to do so," Sydney noted. "However, it can also cause all kinds of headaches and pain. So how to go about living it and making the decisions we all must make isn't always easy, no matter how you look at it."

By the time she was done with Amelia's checkup, Sydney nodded happily. "You are definitely building up some strength, so hopefully that will make everybody happy."

"I would like to think so, but we all know that somebody won't be happy."

"Nope, I understand that," Sydney admitted, "and that's one of the reasons that, the stronger you get, the more we need to be ready for anybody who may react badly to hearing that news."

"Doesn't everybody out there already know I'm improving?" she asked. "How can that news not be all over this area?"

"We've intentionally limited that information," Syndey stated, "because of those earlier attempts on your life."

Meaning, that they believed not everybody would be happy to see her survive, especially the killer. Amelia nodded. "So, as far as everybody else is concerned, my recovery isn't guaranteed."

"Exactly, and it's just a tactic we're using to buy us some time. It's not that we're trying to be dishonest, though some will take it that way and will get angry. Still, others probably won't give a crap either way," Sydney added, with a chuckle.

"I'll go with the don't-give-a-crap route myself," Amelia quipped. "I want to ensure that, when I finally leave this place, I'm in one piece and have a life ahead of me."

"You and me both," Sydney agreed, smiling brightly, "you and me both."

Amelia realized that, for everybody here, a sense of imminent danger remained and was always a possibility where they would be the next victim. Even as victims themselves made no sense of it, sometimes killers didn't make sense either.

When Sydney got a text, she told Amelia that she had to step out into the hallway but that Mountain was on his way. Even with that warning, when a rap came immediately on the clinic door, Amelia stiffened automatically and knew that Sydney sensed it immediately. "It's all right," she told her, as she called out, "Come in."

Instantly Mountain pushed open the door and held it for his brother to enter with a tray.

"So, is that for you or for me?" Amelia asked Mountain and Teegan, with a huge smile.

"It's for both of us," Mountain replied, "if I'm okay to visit and if Sydney approves my dietary choices for you." He looked at Sydney, and she nodded slightly.

"You're okay to visit too, Teegan," Amelia declared, "as long as you had a nap yourself."

He rolled his eyes. "And if I didn't?"

"Then I'll eat alone," Amelia replied immediately, then laughed at the look on Mountain's face.

"Still, I won't be alone," Teegan replied with a smirk, and Amelia laughed at his innuendo.

"And how come I haven't met this lady in your life?" Amelia asked Teegan.

"Because my brother won't let her in here," he stated, with a dirty look aimed at Mountain.

"And yet she belongs here, as I understand," Amelia noted.

"Yes, but security clearance has become an issue."

Then someone else arrived at the door. "I've received my clearance," the woman announced cheerfully, as she walked in. "I'm Sandrine," she introduced herself to the patient, walking over with a smile. "You must be the famous Amelia I've heard so much about. Thank you so very much for keeping Teegan alive."

"You're most welcome," Amelia replied, smiling at the newcomer. She watched as the other woman came over to

Teegan and slipped her arm around his back.

Teegan immediately hugged her gently and looked over at Amelia. "Mountain was pretty specific that we're only allowed a quick visit."

Amelia gave him a small smile. "Not sure whether he's protecting me or trying to keep track of every word that comes out of my mouth," she murmured.

"Both," said Mountain, glaring at her. "And they shouldn't be tiring you out," he added briskly, looking at Amelia.

She gave a half laugh. "How do you know they're tiring me out?"

"Everything does. You say it doesn't, and then, next thing I know, you're sound asleep again." When she glared at him, he nodded. "You think I don't know? I'm watching you," he stated, crossing his arms. "And believe me, I can see how tired you are."

"Maybe," she acknowledged, with a shrug, "but that's just life. I'm healing, and you've got to remember that too," she pointed out.

"You are healing, but it'll take a while. You're not at full strength, and, as long as you're not, you're vulnerable."

"I'm a woman. I'm vulnerable anytime."

He gave her a ghost of a smile. "Actually," Mountain clarified, with an odd expression on his face, "I would pit your chances against half this base. You've got a wariness that I hadn't expected, and your will to live is pretty damn strong. You also have skills that most of the people here don't know how to use, and they don't have the same instincts that go along with Arctic survival rules," he explained, with a shrug. "So, I'm not sure that you're right on that element." She looked at him, surprised at the unexpected compliment, and he nodded. "Regardless, you are to stay here, keep calm, and heal for now."

"So, that's your orders, *huh?*" she asked, with a mocking tone.

He gave her a ghost of a smile again and nodded. Then he looked at the other two and snarled, "Out with the two of you."

Teegan laughed and, with a cheerful look at Amelia, said, "If I didn't know better, the two of you are acting like an old married couple."

Amelia snorted at that, and Mountain glared at him. Teegan said in a loud whisper, as he walked past his brother, "Be nice to her. She's definitely your kind." With that, he was gone, dragging Sandrine out, with her hand in his.

At that, Amelia looked over at Mountain and asked, "You don't have a kind, do you?"

"I try not to. That makes me weak."

"Doesn't make you weak," she scoffed. "It makes you predictable."

Laughing, he nodded. "Yeah, and that would never do either," he declared, with a watchful gaze.

"I guess you raised him on your own, didn't you?"

"He's not that young, but yes. Our parents were not exactly stable, … even at the best of times."

"I can understand that."

He nodded. "You need to get better."

"And you need to find out who did this."

"I'm pretty sure I know," he admitted. "We're just waiting for confirmation."

"Good," she replied, "because it would be nice to not be on constant alert, to at least know which one I should be watching for."

"You will remain on alert for a while because, even if we know, … we still have to find a way to make it an ironclad case," he explained, "and that won't be easy."

She nodded. "In that case, can you get me a cup of coffee?"

"No, I can't," he declined cheerfully, "but I'll text somebody who can."

"Seriously, you can't leave me alone for even that long?"

"No, I sure can't. We've had at least three people killed in this very clinic." He looked over at her with a grim smile. "I'm serious. You won't be alone until this is settled."

She frowned and shifted back on her bed.

Then his phone went off, and he looked down at his screen and swore and immediately stood. "I'll lock the door behind me," he muttered. "Do not leave, and nobody comes in." And, with that, he was gone.

She stared at the door in shock, wondering what the hell was going on that would reverse his position so quickly. It's not as if she could do anything about somebody coming inside in any way. And just as she relaxed and decided to wait for whatever news was breaking, she heard somebody at the door and watched as the handle turned. But it was locked, so nobody could get in, but then to her surprise and ensuing horror, it started to open …

MOUNTAIN RACED TO Elijah's holding place, a small storage room off the kitchen area, and he found Samson there ahead of him. Sydney was working on the prone man at the same time. Mountain swore, as he bent down beside her.

"Don't even ask me questions. I don't know anything yet. I'm hoping to stabilize him and to keep him alive." And, with that, she shoved her fingers down Chef's throat and made the big man throw up all over the floor, and with it came several pills. She nodded. "I wondered if he would try."

"I didn't think he had anything he could try with," Mountain said, staring down at the pills in anger.

"He shouldn't have had access."

"No, but somebody else is playing a game here. You know that. We all know that."

"So do I," she muttered. "We're just not getting to the bottom of it fast enough." She glared at Mountain, but then her gaze softened, as if to say it wasn't his fault.

Mountain nodded. "Is Elijah alive?"

"He is," she confirmed, as she sat back and checked his vitals. "I think we got to him in time." She looked back over at Samson. "Good timing on your part."

He glared down at the prone man. "Not so sure about that. I came down to talk to him. I thought somebody was supposed to be here all the time."

"There is," Mountain declared, as he hopped to his feet and looked around. "Where the hell is Kaylan? He's supposed to be here on guard." He pulled out his phone and made a few calls, but nobody had seen him. Swearing, he muttered, "I'll be right back." He took a quick look around the pantry and kitchen area, then raced outside, without the proper outerwear on, but just to check the generator shed. As he circled around to the kitchen's back door, shivering with the cold, he saw a snow lump around a corner.

He bent down and heaved him up and carried him inside. Samson and Sydney were still focused on Elijah. Then Samson took one look at Mountain, swore and raced over to help him. As they slowly lowered the frozen man to the floor, he looked back at Sydney, and her gaze was shocked and sorrowful as she studied the man in front of him.

"It seems to have been quite a while, but give me a chance." She checked the poor man, as they tried to warm him up. Even after just a handful of minutes, his head trauma was deemed the cause of Kaylan's instant death. While Kaylan was dead, the good news was that Elijah was alive, and, by the looks of it, the chef would survive. He would live to answer questions another day.

As Mountain sat back, he realized how much all of this had gone to shit. He looked over at Samson. "We need to fix this now."

"I know. I'm not arguing with you. I'd hoped for more information though."

Mountain shook his head. "I don't care about information anymore. We'll call his bluff and stop this, and we need to do it before anybody else dies." He stared at Kaylan. "He didn't need to die."

"We weren't really expecting an attack on the guards," Magnus stated from the doorway, as he eyed the dead body. "Did he freeze to death?"

"Looks as if he sustained a severe head injury, which probably would have killed him in the first place," Sydney shared, as she shifted back from the dead man on the floor. "I'll need him moved to the generator shed," she noted, looking back at Mountain.

He nodded, grabbed a blanket from Chef's bed, wrapped up the dead man, and, without a word, straightened up and headed outside again.

Samson looked at him and swore. "Does he ever put on outerwear?"

"Not very often," Magnus replied. "He's got a hell of a lot more body weight than the rest of us."

"He'll still freeze," Samson snapped, as he shook his head. "Christ, the man really is well named, isn't he?"

"He is, but more than that, … he's got the temperament that goes the distance," Sydney shared.

Samson stared at Magnus suddenly. "Sydney, … if you're here, and Mountain is here, … where the hell is Amelia?"

Mountain called out from the doorway, "I called Teegan to stay with her, but I'm heading back there now." And, with that, he cast one glance around and bolted back to Amelia. As soon as he entered the medical clinic, Teegan was still searching this room, while pulling out his phone.

"I've looked everywhere," he stated. "She's not here."

Immediately Mountain initiated a full alert, looking for Amelia. As the whole base bolted into action, Mountain turned in the hallway, wide-eyed, and looked at Samson, who ran to join him.

"She can't be far," Samson noted. "She can't walk very easily herself, not for much distance."

"Let's check the bathrooms first," Mountain suggested, coming up behind him, "and then fan out. Somebody could have stashed her in a bathroom or any bedroom, if she didn't leave on her own, particularly if Teegan came very quickly."

"I was right here, so they didn't have more than a few minutes."

Mountain didn't waste any time. He took one side of the hallway, and Samson took the other. Mountain bolted into the first bathroom, checked it, and found nothing. By the time he headed to the last room on his side of the hallway, his heart was slamming against his chest, a full-blown panic setting in. He opened the door, and there she was, crumpled on the floor, unconscious. He let out a roar that had the rest of the nearby search group racing toward him.

Sydney pushed past him and bent to check Amelia and nodded. "She's alive. Let's get her back onto the hospital bed, so I can take a look at any injuries."

Mountain brushed aside everybody, then bent down and scooped up Amelia, with the ease of somebody well used to lifting much heavier loads, and carried her back to the medical clinic. As he walked in, Magnus and Berry were bringing Chef over. With both of the patients now ensconced in the clinic, Mountain swore, as he stared down at Amelia. "What if it was all a ruse?"

"It wasn't a ruse, but it was good timing," Samson suggested, beside him. "I get that you think you were called away in order to get at Amelia, and maybe that was part of it," he conceded. "However, you also have to understand that the attack on Elijah was real."

"But was it an attack or did he do it himself? In which case, it wouldn't have involved Amelia." Mountain shook his head.

"I hear what you're saying, and I know that's still potentially an option, but I'm going with the fact that somebody killed our guard, took out Elijah, and had enough time to come snag Amelia. All he had to do was get her out that same damn exit, and we wouldn't have found her in time," Samson noted.

He looked over at Sydney. "Is she hurt?"

"Not sure, and I wonder if she's been drugged again," she muttered, swearing, "not pills though."

"So why didn't they do that to Elijah? Why didn't they

do that to Kaylan?"

"Maybe, for the guard, they did," she noted, looking back at him. "Maybe he didn't succumb as easily to the head trauma. Maybe he fought for his life," she suggested. "No way to know yet. I'll need some time to check out his body. However, at the moment, I have to deal with the warm bodies and ensure they stay that way." Sydney shook her head, when Samson tried to say something. "I've got to keep them alive," she stated, "and right about now you guys are not helping."

Teegan stared from the back of the room. "He didn't have five minutes," he snapped. "You contacted me, and I was already on my feet, racing this way." He shook his head. "Honestly there was maybe seven minutes at the most that Amelia was alone," he cried out. "There's no way."

"And yet"—Mountain stopped and looked back, as if at the bedroom he'd found her in—"that was an empty room, and she was in there. So our suspect knew it was an empty room. Who would know what rooms are empty?"

Magnus looked at him intently. "Almost everybody on this base," he said. "No way to keep something like that quiet, really. Even if somebody had gone looking for an empty room, they would have found one quite easily."

"But who would have known ahead of time?" Mountain asked.

Magnus sighed. "Chances are the killer would have known ahead of time, but that doesn't mean he didn't figure it out on the fly or didn't have it tucked away in the back of his mind. All he needed to do was physically check the rooms quickly, or, if he knew ahead of time, maybe that was an opportunity not to be missed."

"What about the cameras?"

At that, Barret showed up, holding cameras in his hand. "Ripped out," he noted.

"So, somebody who knew about the cameras, though that's really not a surprise," Mountain stated, turning to face Samson.

Samson nodded. "Unfortunately too many people know too much around here."

"At this point, yes," Mountain agreed.

At that moment, Elijah groaned and shifted.

Mountain immediately walked over, trying to stop the big man from rolling off the bed. Quickly gathering up the straps, Mountain secured him. When Chef opened his gaze and started to resist, Mountain calmed him down immediately, hands on his shoulders, pressing firmly down, explaining what had happened.

Finally, Elijah settled back and stared up at him. "I didn't take those pills," he said, his voice harsh.

Mountain shrugged. "They were in your stomach, so I'm not sure how else they would have gotten there."

Chef frowned. "They were supposed to be painkillers. My head was killing me," he shared, as he looked over at Sydney. "Didn't you give them to him?"

"Give them to whom? Who is *him*?" Sydney asked Elijah.

At that, his gaze narrowed, and he clammed up.

Mountain gave him a hard shake. "That's enough of this bullshit. You need to say his name. You need to speak up and tell me who gave you those pills."

He looked over at him, dazed. "Kaylan."

"Yeah, well, as much as I would like to believe you, Kaylan lost his life. Whether he was drugged first or not, he was hit hard over the head with some blunt force instrument that likely would have killed him immediately. Then he was dragged outside, where he froze to death for good measure," Mountain bellowed, almost roaring in the chef's face. "Another innocent man has died, this time trying to keep you alive."

At that, Elijah glared at him. "Then don't keep me alive," he roared right back, and his voice broke. "I don't fucking deserve it."

At that, Mountain sat back and looked at him intently. "I won't argue that point right now, but you and I aren't done." Mountain was so angry that he knew he needed to take a step back. He looked down at Chef Elijah, who had rolled over onto his side, his eyes closed.

Sydney stood protectively over him.

"Yeah, I'm walking away for the moment. I get it." He held up his hands, as Sydney dragged him away from Chef. "You call me. … As soon as Amelia wakes up, you call me." He headed out the door but turned and glared at her. "Do you hear me?"

"She'll be fine," Sydney replied gently. "I know it's another big scare, but we saved her this time."

"We saved her," Mountain repeated, "but Kaylan? … He was a young man, … about twenty-seven years old. *He* didn't make it," Mountain declared, his voice haunted. "Enough is enough."

And, with that, he bolted from the room.

A MELIA WOKE UP, feeling a dryness in her mouth and a headache that she hadn't felt in a long time. She tried to work up some moisture in order to swallow, but it seemed almost impossible. A moment later, a straw was placed between her lips, and she sucked eagerly, raising her eyelids to see Sydney. She croaked out, "That … doesn't feel very good."

"You were attacked again," Sydney explained, sitting down on the chair beside her patient.

Amelia's eyes widened at that announcement. "I was what?" she asked, blinking at her. "Are you sure?"

"Oh, we're sure. We found you were taken a few rooms away, … unless you got up and bolted on your own. Did you leave the clinic?"

"Bolted?" she repeated, and then her gaze cleared. "Actually the door opened," she said, trying to get her thoughts together. "Mountain had been here and got a text. Before he left, he told me not to leave the room, saying that the door was locked, and he would be back. He didn't give me any other explanation, and he ran off," she shared, taking a short breath, "but then, almost immediately, the door opened."

She frowned, confused. "It was supposed to be locked. It opened, and then it stopped, and I heard some voices up and down the hallway. I slipped out of the bed and hid behind the door," she said, holding her side.

"I was surprised that I could walk as well as I could, and yet … I was so scared, and my heart was hammering against my chest—to the point that I was sure anybody coming in could hear that. And then … someone whispered from the other side of the door."

"What did they say?" Sydney asked.

"It was hard to hear, but he basically said, *I'm coming for you, maybe not now, maybe not tonight, but I'm coming for you.* And then I heard running footsteps. I stepped out into the hallway to try and find him, but several people were in the hallway, and they looked at me oddly, and then they all scattered, as if some warning went out." She took a deep breath.

Sydney took Amelia's hand in hers. "Go on."

"I wanted to follow, to see who was running away," she explained, "and I started down the hallway, but I wasn't feeling very well. By the time I got down to the far side of the hallway, I thought I was going inside the bathroom, but I was in an empty bedroom. Just as I opened the door, stepped in, and shut the door behind me, the floor rushed up to hit me in the face."

"It rushed up and hit you all right," Sydney confirmed, "but I'm relieved to think that nobody carried you down there."

"I don't think so," Amelia muttered. "I was heading to see what was going on, and I was determined to let Mountain know that someone had been right there talking to me. Whoever he was, he knew I was behind the door, Sydney. It was as if he was laughing at me." Amelia's whole body shook. "It was scary. Honest to God, he was pretty damn scary."

"Anybody who's stalking us, threatening us, they have

the upper hand because they're not afraid, and they know what they can do to terrorize us. Meanwhile, we are afraid, especially not knowing who our true enemy is. Sometimes our imagination is worse than the reality. Still, once we're afraid, we become a victim," Sydney pointed out, "and they immediately gain the upper hand."

Amelia stared at her and slowly nodded. "It was just like that, as if he wanted me to be afraid, to know that he was coming for me, and to be terrorized by it," she said. "Who the hell does that?"

"All kinds of people do it, and none of them are nice," Sydney pointed out. "The bottom line is, we have you back, safe and sound."

"What was the emergency about that had Mountain running from here?" Amelia asked.

Sydney pointed to the second hospital bed, behind Amelia's. "Either Elijah was attacked, or he chose to take pills on his own," she shared. "We got to him fast enough to save him. We're not exactly sure of the details yet, but, in the process, his guard was murdered."

"Murdered?" Amelia repeated, staring nervously at the doc.

"Yes, probably by the same person talking to you. Is there anything you can tell me about his voice?"

"No," she replied, "nothing concrete anyway. Plus, other people were in the hallway, making it hard to hear the voice. But it was scary, this raw, hoarse whisper that I'll never forget."

"No, and maybe not forgetting is a good thing," Sydney said, "because you're alive right now. I don't know whether they came to this room after you, and your hiding in that bedroom helped you, or if they drugged you and put you there. However, you're alive, and we want to keep it that way."

"And yet it feels very much as if, the longer I stay here, the less chance I have of staying alive," she admitted, staring at her. "Dear God, surely the investigators know now who's behind this?"

Mountain strolled back in again, accompanied by Samson, and Mountain looked at her sternly. "Report."

She rolled her eyes. "I can answer questions, but I don't take orders very well." He glared at her, and she smiled. "Somehow I feel you're upset at yourself because you left me. I don't know if he intended this misdirection, but—" Then she quickly told him what happened.

Mountain frowned. "So, you weren't drugged? You took yourself down to that bedroom on your own, presumably because you thought that he was out there?"

"I don't know. … I thought that maybe I could find out who he was and put this all to an end or figure out what all the commotion was about at least. I went out and headed down the hallway—not my smartest move, I'm sure."

"So, did you see him at all?" Mountain asked, Samson silently listening.

Amelia shook her head. "I heard him run away, so I was looking for a man running. Many other people were out there in the hallway, but none were running. Among the chaos, I didn't see just one person but many. If he did come back to the clinic, I wasn't there for him to torment anymore. Whether he was planning on doing that or not, I don't know." She raised her hands in frustration. "That's all I remember."

Mountain nodded thoughtfully and didn't say anything for a long moment, as he stared at her. "How are you feeling?" he asked gently.

"Rough, about what you would expect, I guess. If I hadn't fallen or collapsed or whatever it was that I did," she added, with a note of humor, "I would probably feel a whole lot better, but I did fall, so *yay me*. ... I've got a bit of a headache now."

"Yeah, that would happen when you collapse," Sydney replied, with a note of relief in her voice.

"The good news is, I'm alive." Amelia gave a nod and a smile in the doc's direction. "Are we any closer to figuring out what the hell is going on?" she asked Mountain.

"Oh, yeah. We're closer, but, so far, nobody is willing to say anything that will bust this thing wide open. I need Elijah awake now," Mountain muttered, as he turned toward the man on the other hospital bed, seemingly asleep.

MOUNTAIN WALKED OVER and stared down at Chef. "Old man, are you finally ready to tell us something, or will you let more young men die because of your actions and inactions?"

Elijah didn't say anything, but his body stiffened visibly, confirming to Mountain that Chef had heard.

"You heard what Amelia told us, right? About somebody tormenting her, wanting to kill her, wanting to hurt her, after she had done nothing but save Teegan," Mountain stated. "When is *enough* really enough for you? How much bloodshed must be spread before you finally admit this needs to stop? When do you stop protecting this killer?" Mountain roared, his temper getting the best of him.

Elijah looked up at him in resignation and nodded.

"Now. I guess now."

"Damn right, so tell me who the hell is doing this."

Mountain and Samson, with permission from Sydney, moved Chef to Sydney's private quarters next door, so they would have some privacy.

"You already know," Chef stated, as they settled in Sydney's bedroom. "That's why you're so angry because you don't know how to stop it. I didn't know how to stop it either, so I did the next best thing and made sure he didn't ever do it while I was around."

"Sure, but that didn't stop the killing though, did it?"

"No, it's not something I could stop," he repeated.

"What started it up again?" he asked.

Elijah looked at him. "A whole lot of things, but, in reality, it was pretty simple."

"Then we're heading to a more private place." Together Mountain and Samson moved Elijah to their office. As soon as he was seated, Elijah started to talk, unwinding the tale of blood and gore.

EXHAUSTED FROM HER venture down the hallway and her collapse on the floor, Amelia sat up in her hospital bed, willing her headache to go away, not willing to take anything for it. She still thought about that voice, that harsh whisper, that person on the other side of the door, knowing that she was there, knowing that she was terrified. It sent chills down her spine every time she thought of it, and yet she couldn't help herself.

How did one stop thinking about something like that? Just so much was wrong with the whole idea of somebody actively taking pleasure in her terror, and yet that's what it was. He had been thrilled, absolutely thrilled with the knowledge that she had been hiding from him, without even knowing who he was. She didn't even think she'd ever heard that voice before. Yet, as a whisper, it was impossible to really know.

Sydney was still at her desk, and Magnus had already come and gone several times. Amelia knew she wouldn't be alone ever again, at least not while this was going on. However, she knew in her gut that her stalker would make an attempt and that he was somebody with enough skill and experience to pull it off. And that was what he was after. She didn't have a clue when or how that attack would come, but it would.

That was the part that terrified her the most.

She kept looking around, and every movement, every sound, made her jump, as she sat up in bed. Even now she couldn't lie down and relax because it would take an extra few seconds to get up out of the bed and get moving, should her attacker come again.

Finally having enough of it, Sydney walked over and put a hand on Amelia's shoulder. "Hey, look. Do you need something to help you to relax?"

She looked at her, firmed her bottom lip, and shook her head. "Honest to God, I would much rather go out where the dogs are now."

Sydney's eyebrows shot up. "To see your dogs?" she asked, then smiled, and clearly it came from the heart.

"I would absolutely love to see them," Amelia murmured. "Surely I'm strong enough to see them now."

"I don't know."

"And, if I can't go over to the dogs, maybe the dogs could come here?" she asked hopefully. At that, Sydney nodded and pulled out her phone. "I'll see what I can do about it. We've had an awful lot of dogs throughout the place at various times, but we haven't had yours over because I didn't want you moving about that much."

"I have four," Amelia clarified.

Sydney turned to her, startled, then nodded. "Of course. That's what you need to pull a sled, I suppose."

"Joe knows which ones are mine," she said, with a smile. "It's not as if he'll mistake them."

"Good enough," Sydney replied, then took several steps away and spoke into her phone but in a low voice, so nothing could be overheard. It was disconcerting for Amelia to think that everybody was watching her, walking around her, always trying to keep her safe, controlling everything that went on in her world. It was not how she wanted to live at all.

If she could escape right now, she would, and, for the first time, she recognized that budding sense of fear, that ever-building sense of terror, of wrongness, around this place—knowing a villain was here, a boogeyman ready to jump out. If that weren't enough, imagining that poor guard's body, knowing he had been found dead out in the cold, was enough to make her understand how adamant Teegan had been about not returning to this military base. Amelia now knew because something was very wrong and because somebody would try and kill him. Now her too.

Obviously somebody had already tried to kill Teegan, and it was a matter of Amelia's keeping him alive that had saved him. Still, even now she knew Teegan wasn't safe, but, hell, she wasn't either. She doubted any of them were. Whatever was happening, whatever was going on here, just made this killer more ambitious, more frenzied, and, in many ways, maybe more prone to make mistakes.

He was moving faster and taking chances. There was no need to threaten her, no need to make her scared and do that behind-the-door number he had done, except that he was tormenting her, taunting her, as if he didn't give a damn, as if the world was breaking apart, and he didn't want anything to do with it. How the hell was that even a thing?

She shook her head, as she stared off in the distance, her mind thinking about doors, locks, access, and the fact that so many people were here who could have access to absolutely everything. So many who dressed the same, so many of similar size, similar shape, and similar physical condition. She quickly discarded the other women because it hadn't been a woman's voice; and the people of note that she'd seen out in the wilderness hadn't been women either. Sure, some men here were smaller in stature, but certainly nobody was as small as the women here that Amelia had seen and met, and that's what made the difference.

So, no. Amelia was pretty damn sure the killer was a male.

That left what? Twenty-two or so men to choose from on base? She snorted at that, because twenty-two men who had a room in this military base had all kinds of time over the last several weeks to access and to copy keys, doing whatever they wanted at any point in time to enter the locked clinic or the locked armory. She couldn't believe it was Elijah, and yet he had the best access of all, as did the day sergeant and the colonel, yet that made the least sense.

If the colonel wanted to kill people, he could give the orders for all kinds of exercise training and arrange for it to go wrong. Under those circumstances, however, it could end up being a mass killing. Surely, if the colonel was really worried about his record, nobody would overlook a mass shooting event easily. Friendly fire was one thing, when it involved a solo victim. But to explain several deaths at once as friendly fire? She shook her head. No, she was pretty sure it wasn't anything like that.

If Sydney weren't the only doctor here on base, Amelia would have immediately suspected the doctor, like those angels of mercy who murdered people because they could or who made it look as if somebody was having a major life event, only to come and seemingly rescue them. Sometimes the rescue worked, and they looked to be a hero, and sometimes the rescue didn't work, and yet they still seemed to be a hero because they'd given it their all. However, in essence, they'd killed the very victim they had supposedly been trying to save.

Of course that brought up many more examples of that serial killer craziness and just depressed Amelia even more. But at least now she seemed more capable of shifting on the bed and stretching out cautiously, until she had her head on the pillow. She wasn't hungry, but she also needed food—fuel. She wasn't thirsty, but she knew she needed water—to avoid dehydration.

What she really needed was to get out of here and to feel better, to feel in some way as if she would get through this. That damn threatening, taunting whisper slipped through her mind again, causing the hairs on the back of her neck to rise. How had he created words so devious, so evil sounding, preying on her fears? He preyed on what she already knew about the base, preyed on the fact that other people had died.

As far as he was concerned, she was next.

When the door to the clinic opened a little later, her gaze zinged to the person who entered, fear sliding through her, even as she desperately tried to control it. But a *woof* coming from the doorway had her bolting upright, only to cry out in pain, sagging back again, as she held a hand to her side.

Sydney immediately raced over to her. "Hey, hey, hey, take it easy. None of that."

"Right," she murmured, "none of that, a little bit too late."

"Yeah, you're not kidding," Sydney agreed, with a chuckle.

Amelia looked over to see Magnus walking her four dogs toward her, all wiggling in joy, while he struggled to keep them in check. Tears in her eyes, she reached out an arm and called to Bandy. Bandy immediately came over and put his two front paws up on the bed and whined at her. She cuddled him gently, his tail wagging like crazy, as she gave him the greetings and cuddles they both longed for. Bandy was very much a cuddlier, wanted that affection, and would have suffered the most from not being around her.

She called Rocket next, who came up on the other side of her bed, waited a second, and, ignoring her, jumped up on the bed and laid down, his head dropping on her chest. She cuddled him too, whispering to him softly. Then Magnus brought the other two over, and immediately Jackson took over Bandy's spot, looking for his own cuddles. By the time she had a chance to cuddle Max, the tears were flowing freely from Amelia's eyes. She looked up at Magnus and whispered, "Thank you."

He nodded. "It's not just about you. I think the dogs are a whole lot better off seeing that you're okay."

She smiled, her hands going from one snout to the other, as she bopped their noses one by one, laughing at their antics. "We've been very close," she murmured, "and it breaks my heart to even be apart from them like this."

"You're on the mend," Magnus stated, "so the good news is, they won't have to do without you for long."

She chuckled. "And yet, if you're a dog owner, you would know that any separation is too long."

"Oh, yes." He chuckled. "That I can understand. However, they have absolutely loved being out there with Joe and his dogs."

"That's good. They're all very social," she shared, "and they've met many times before."

Magnus looked over at her. "That's a surprise."

She frowned at him and asked, "Why? I may be a research scientist, but I love being outside. I probably spend more time with Mother Nature than I do with inputting the data into my laptop. So me and my dogs have seen your dogs out and about. We don't interrupt any training maneuvers, but, when you guys take breaks, I sometimes approach, especially once I figure out who the dog wrangler is in the bunch."

She smiled, still reaching out to all her dogs. "You know how it is with animals. We stop to talk to the dogs and end up meeting the humans. So we've met some people, talked to them. I've seen Joe outside often enough. Elijah too. Remember. I'm up here often, so I've run across Joe and Elijah several times over the years. I just never know if they are back here until I scout out things. Joe takes the dogs out for runs and his own training too," she added, "Honestly, I've seen all of Joe's dogs at various times during the last three months."

"Understandable."

"The dogs know each other, so this must be like a holiday for them, a chance to go visiting for a longer term," she shared, as she scratched their ears, absolutely loving being reunited, her heart overwhelmed with joy at seeing her animals looking so good. "Please give my thanks to Joe for taking such good care of them."

"Oh, he was pretty protective and wanted to confirm these guys were coming here to see you and no one else," Magnus shared, with a smile. "He said he would tag along behind me." Turning to look at the open door, he frowned. "He's supposed to be right behind me."

She laughed. "He probably stopped to say hello to Elijah," she guessed, with a smile. "Those two have been friends since forever."

Magnus turned to face her, frowning.

She nodded. "You didn't know? He, the colonel, and Elijah have been around together many times, at many training facilities and missions of all different kinds." Then she snorted. "Joe has so many stories to tell about those three. Joe's sister was Chef's wife."

Magnus slowly shook his head. "I knew some of it, but what threw me off was how the hell did *you* know all that?"

She looked at him in surprise. "Because I knew Joe, and our family have gotten dogs from him over the last what? … Fifteen, maybe twenty years? Many times he talked about his brother-in-law, who was a chef, so it didn't take long to put it together when I was up here this time. … Can't believe you didn't know."

He stared at her, dumbfounded. "It must be in the files, but people marry, change names," he said, with a shrug. "I thought I asked Chef about Joe."

"Since Chef's wife died, Joe's sister, maybe they haven't been all that close," she suggested. "Some people find solace in sharing the memories, but others just can't deal with remembering. Then after Chef lost his son, that was another whole deal."

"Yeah. I know that the colonel tried his best to keep Chef's son alive, moving him to an easier post."

She frowned at him. "What are you talking about?"

He frowned too, then replied, "According to what Elijah said, the colonel went out of his way to try and save his boy's life by transferring him to a safe area to keep him alive."

"That seems odd because I recall Joe telling me how Chef had talked to his son, and he was headed for the front lines. We had that conversation more than once. Joe's nephew was something we would always visit about."

"The front lines wouldn't be safe," Magnus said, staring at her.

She shrugged. "I don't understand either, but I don't know the details of any of this," she replied. "I did want to ask something though." She glanced over at Sydney and then lowered her voice and asked Magnus, "Is Mountain a really good guy?"

He gave her a gentle smile. "One of the best. If you're heading down that pathway, know that you'll be safe."

She winced. "Yeah? He's got a hell of a temper."

"We all do, including you," he noted, with a tilt of his head. "It's what keeps us alive sometimes. It's that great determination and anger that makes us push ahead, push past the lines where everybody else would have stopped and given up. It's how you kept Teegan alive because you were damned if you would let anybody at this base take him out."

She winced. "You guys thought about that, *huh?*"

"Of course," he said, with a nod. "It's also what we would do. When you're responsible for somebody, responsible for anybody like that, you do what you can, consequences be damned. Yet you still need that temper, you need that fire, because it's the drive that keeps you moving in the right direction, even when all else fails. And, when you're at your weakest point, and you're ready to give up, it's temper that motivates you."

"That is true enough."

"Yeah, it is. If you can push that temper forward," he shared, "it will keep you alive. So don't hate your temper, just understand where it's coming from and that it's often cloaking fear. You can use it to defeat the fear as well."

"I can't imagine Mountain being afraid of anything."

"You didn't see him when Teegan was missing," Magnus shared, his voice low, "because Mountain was beside himself, going out every day to search for hours. Gradually he pulled an entire team together to figure out what was happening here. The fact that we're really close right now, really close to nailing who did all this, is very important," he stated. "The last, maybe thirteen weeks, have been a combination of intensive searching and research and investigation and collaboration."

"Are you … close?"

"Yes. We all really hate the fact that another young man died before we could stop it, and we're desperate to get it stopped before any more deaths happen. So I understand you hid after you heard a man's voice behind the door."

She nodded. "Yes, and he was taunting me, teasing me. Unfortunately he got to me. If I could do anything to get out of here right now, believe me, you would not see my shadow. If I thought I could do it alone," she added, with a shake of her head, "my dogs and I would be long gone."

His gaze narrowed, as he considered that, and he nodded. "I understand why you would feel that way, but I hope you don't try to run on us because we wouldn't have any way of knowing whether you were alive or dead. Plus, after what Mountain's already been through, that would devastate him." When she looked at him in surprise, he nodded. "Don't tell me that you can't see the same attraction."

She flushed and bowed her head. "It's hardly the right situation or timing for that."

"No, and yet you saved his brother, and, for that, he will always look at you differently."

"Yeah, but I don't want him to look at me with just some sense of gratitude," she muttered in disgust. "That sounds fundamentally wrong and bound to fail."

He burst out laughing. "I've heard that a time or two, but usually from the men," he admitted, with a smile. "Can't say I've ever thought of it coming from a woman." She glared at him, and, raising his hands in peace, he added, "I'm not trying to be sexist. I know several guys who have been in that position, where they'd become a hero on some occasion and never wanted the damsel in distress to look at them with that air of gratitude because, to them, it clouded their judgment."

"Exactly," she agreed, with a careless shrug and winced at the pain in her side. "If Mountain is interested in a relationship, he better be interested in a relationship with me, not because of what went on to save Teegan."

"And how do you feel about Mountain?"

"Wary," she replied immediately, "and yet not. He was there for me for several days and nights, when I was in and out, not exactly alive, if you know what I mean. I also knew about him well ahead of time, since Teegan rattled on about him constantly," she said, with a knowing smile.

When Magnus looked at her in surprise, she nodded.

"It was *Mountain this* and *Mountain that*. At first I didn't understand and thought it was all fever-induced ramblings, until finally, through all the meanderings," she admitted, with a light chuckle, "I figured out that Mountain was a person. Once I realized it was a person, it didn't take too much more to figure out that he was a brother of the superhero variety and a very large influence in Teegan's life."

"Very much so," Magnus confirmed.

"He also mentioned something about Mason, but I didn't understand that."

Magnus chuckled. "Mason is a mutual friend, a good

friend of this base," he stated. "Several of us have heard all these stories about Mason, and, as far as I'm concerned, he and Mountain are both legitimate heroes."

"I'm glad to hear it," she said. "I wasn't exactly sure what I was getting myself into, both when I brought Teegan here or when I came in myself. Yet I didn't have any choice. At some point in time you have to accept help, even if you're afraid it's the wrong thing."

"Sometimes it is, but, in this case, … you made the right choice. Please promise me that you won't run and leave us wondering what happened to you. That would be the worst thing you could do. It's also quite possible that your scary visitor said what he did in order to spook you into running. Did you consider that?"

Startled, she shook her head. "I can't say that I did."

"It's quite possible," he noted, "and that would be another thing to watch out for because, if you do run, he could be right out there, waiting for you."

She winced and then nodded. "That's not a possibility I want to consider either. I could keep the dogs here with me though." She looked up at him hopefully, her gaze going over to Sydney, then back to Magnus. He frowned at her thoughtfully, and she realized he was considering it. She beamed. "Nobody'll get to me if I've got them by my side," she pointed out excitedly. "Having them in here will stop anybody from coming at me."

"Or will get them shot."

The smile immediately dropped from her face, and her heart sank. "Oh, God, … you're right. … Better to take them back. They'll have a good life with Joe, even if I don't make it through this."

"Whoa, whoa, whoa," Sydney interjected, coming over

to her immediately. "None of that talk." She glared at Magnus, then back at Amelia. "We won't tolerate any of that talk. Pick two dogs, not all four."

She looked at her and asked, "Seriously?"

"Yes, seriously. Pick the ones most likely to protect you and not to lick an intruder to bits."

"It depends," Amelia muttered, "but you're right." Then she quickly chose Jackson and Bandy. She gave the other two big cuddles, saying goodbye.

Magnus walked them to the door, leaving the other two with her. The two dogs went with him willingly, as he reached a hand down to cuddle them. When they stepped out of the clinic, several people in the hallway wanted to say hi to the dogs. She watched them in the doorway, as several people cuddled the dogs, but she kept these two very close to her bed. Several people looked into the medical clinic, saw the other dogs, and she called out, "Please don't approach. They aren't friendly."

They stopped dead in their tracks. One nodded and replied, "I guess that's a good warning, but I'm surprised, considering he's in here."

She smiled but didn't say anything.

As soon as he left, Sydney looked over at her intently. "Are they dangerous?"

"No, not at all. I just don't want anybody coming in here making friends with these two, not if the whole point of this is to keep me safe," she explained, looking at Sydney with a wry look. "Not that I don't trust people, but …"

Sydney gave her a hard look. "Don't trust anybody here," she declared. "Honest to God, until we know what's going on, let's keep the dogs separated, and let's make sure that people don't come in here. We were trying to keep your condition a secret, but the fact that you were up and around and moving has caused a certain amount of renewed interest." She stood with her hands on her hips regarding her. "Good thing I took the catheter out beforehand. You could have hurt yourself even more."

"Of course, but obviously I'm still not quite capable of heading out and running, although if it came to a choice between that and something else," she muttered, "believe me. I would be long gone."

"Got it." Sydney nodded, then walked to a small cubicle and pulled out Amelia's clothes. "Having said that, I do think that Magnus had a point about somebody hoping you'll try to jackrabbit out of here. Here's what we have of your clothes. They are washed and salvageable. I didn't have to cut anything off because they were so loose on you."

"Yeah, I'd lost a fair bit of weight, so pretty much everything I had was getting baggy," she replied, with a wry look. "I am quite grateful to have clothes." She got up and slowly walked several steps around the room. "Even after falling and my short trip down the hall, I feel stronger. Just something about being on your own is so uplifting."

Sydney gave her a commiserating smile. "Absolutely," she agreed, with a laugh. "Teegan mentioned the same thing not that long ago."

She looked down at her clothes and once again settled on her bed, her clothing nearby. When a ruckus came at the door, the dogs immediately stood at attention, and Bandy barked. Amelia placed a hand on their collars, as the door opened, and Joe stepped in. Then immediately the two dogs surged toward him.

He smiled, looked over at her, and nodded. "I guess this is where the missing two dogs are. How are you doing today?"

"I'm doing fine, thank you," she replied, with a nod and a beaming smile. "Thank you so much for looking after my dogs."

He nodded and didn't seem to be too bothered, as he was on his knees, hugging both of the dogs. "They're mighty fine animals," he declared, looking at her, "and you've done a good job with them."

"Even when we were a little short on supplies," she admitted, with an eye roll.

He chuckled. "They aren't suffering, and they've been tanking up pretty well now, while they've been here." He eyed her critically and added, "Looks as if your dogs are doing a better job at that than you are."

"I am starting to get a decent appetite," she shared, "but I lost a lot of weight this last month."

He nodded. "That's what living out in the north tundra will do to you. You need to put on that blubber, not lose it."

"Not a whole lot of blubber on me to begin with," she noted, with a smirk.

He smiled, then turned around to look at the place. "Are you keeping the dogs in here?" he asked in some confusion, then asked Sydney, "Is that wise, considering it's a medical clinic?"

"Just for the night," Sydney noted.

He hesitated and then nodded. "That's fine then," he said, as he stepped out. "I'll make sure the other two are taken care of." He looked around intently. "Where are they, anyway?"

"Magnus took them back to the dog barn," Amelia replied. "And I really do appreciate all the care you're giving them." He held up a hand and waved, then quickly stepped out the door. As soon as he was gone, Amelia was filled with a sense of disquiet and turned to Sydney. "You do realize that, if the dogs have already made friends with somebody from the base, I'm the furthest thing from being safe with them here."

Sydney nodded, a shadow crossing her face. "Are you talking about Joe, or are you talking about any of the million people who have been through his quarters and all the care that they've given to the dogs? So much so that *any* of the dogs know all the men and your dogs now too."

"That's the trouble," she agreed, with a shrug. "If anybody wanted to make friends with the dogs, particularly so they could get close to me, we gave them the means to do so. And not only did we give them the means to do so, they also have the means to get close to me. These dogs not only won't stop them, they'll probably welcome them. I kept the two most defensive guarders of the four, but, seeing their reaction to Joe right now, it won't make a damn bit of difference if they're here or not."

And, with that, she got up and determinedly started dressing.

Sydney walked over and asked, "What are you planning?"

She shook her head and said in a confused tone, "I don't know, but I can't stay here."

"Why? Why now?"

"Here in this clinic, I'm a sitting duck. I'm on the pond, and they're on the shore, but this pond is pretty damn shallow. Even without a weapon they can reach me," Amelia explained. "I need a place to hide, and I need to go there fast."

Sydney nodded. "Let me help you." She quickly reached

for her clothing and helped her get them on. Then she called Magnus to send someone to return Bandy and Jackson back to the dog barn.

MOUNTAIN OPENED THE door to Elijah's *cell* for Samson. "You need to hear this." He tried hard to keep the urgency out of his voice, but, damn it, this was what they'd been waiting for, and they needed action right now. He shut the door, as he looked back at Elijah. "Is Amelia in any danger?"

Chef shrugged. "I don't know anymore," he admitted miserably. "Ever since we came up here, things have gone crazy."

Mountain turned to Samson, eyeing him. "I'm surprised to see you down here."

"Are you, though?" Samson asked, with half a smile. "When the shit hits the fan, usually those of us who are used to dealing with shit get called in to help."

Elijah nodded slowly. "I really did try."

"I'm sure you did," Samson replied, as he sat down. He looked over at Mountain, who even now found it hard to control his pacing. "What's the matter with you?"

"Amelia. I get the feeling something is wrong."

He looked at him and then shrugged. "So, what the hell are you doing here then? Elijah can talk to me without you here. You already have the information, but I don't. So, as long as it's safe, get yourself out of here."

And, with that, Mountain nodded. He turned and looked at Elijah, who just waved him off. "Yeah, yeah, go on. Don't let that girl die. She's good people."

"She is good people," Mountain confirmed, as he bolted

from the room. He raced to the medical clinic. He noted Magnus taking two dogs down the hallway, and the clinic door was open. Sydney stood in the hallway, watching Magnus leave, while rubbing her arms. Seeing her there, Mountain calmed down immediately. "Hey," he said.

"Hey," she replied, then took a deep breath. "She didn't feel safe. She wanted to leave."

"Oh no, no, no," he cried out, but then immediately lowered his voice, as he had attracted attention from others in the hallway. "Where did she go?" he asked urgently, pulling the doc back inside the clinic and shutting the door behind them.

She quickly explained the conversation they'd had about the dogs and the fact that Amelia felt like a sitting duck in the clinic. "She told me that she'll find a place to hide in the compound, and, if that didn't work, she was leaving."

"How the hell will she hide here?"

She gave him half a smile. "I asked her that, and she shook her head and told me that it was better if I didn't know. As she left, she told me, *Mountain will know.*" He frowned at her, but Sydney added, "I'm really hoping that's true."

He shook his head, but his mind raced through various possibilities. "What condition is she in to handle the cold?" he whispered, not wanting others to hear.

"Not good enough," she stated bluntly. "Not unless it was an absolute life-and-death emergency and the only other choice."

"Did she really think it was that bad?"

"I think we should trust her instincts, so I helped her get dressed. It was clear she would do it anyway," she shared, throwing up her hands in frustration. "Magnus was worried about this earlier and had warned her that the killer's taunts to scare her could well have been intended to spook her into running. She understood that intellectually, but she didn't feel safe in the clinic. At that point, I knew I couldn't keep her here without an altercation, so I told her that she needed to find a place inside the base, where she felt safe. She agreed but noted there weren't many places like that. Still, she thought she might know of one."

"How?" he asked. "She's been unconscious in the clinic most of her time here and only just recently walked down the hallway." He shook his head, growing more frustrated. He didn't have a clue what space could even possibly be considered safe in the base right now. "Anybody else come by?" he asked hesitantly.

She shook her head. "There's been a steady activity of people in the hall today. There were several when Magnus came through with the dogs, then again as Joe came to see about the two missing dogs. Later, when we opened the door to let Amelia out, a couple glanced our way and kept on walking. She waited until it was completely clear before she left."

"Which direction?"

She gave him a ghost of a smile and pointed. He was gone instantly and now he wished he had a dog to track Amelia. She seemed to think he would know wherever the hell she had gone to hide, and that blew him away, since he didn't know her that well. Yet part of him realized that he absolutely did. He knew what she was like. He knew how well she had protected his brother and had looked after herself, so where the hell would she go?

Then he had a flash and stopped, shook his head, and pondered this thought, as he slowly changed course. As he approached his own quarters, he hesitated, then, without warning, stepped inside and closed the door quickly behind him.

There she was, curled up in his bed, sound asleep.

"Jesus Christ," he muttered.

She blinked her eyes open. "I'm not sleeping, honest."

"Yeah, you were," he countered, with a smile on his face and tenderness in his heart. "After that much exertion? … Getting dressed and leaving the clinic exhausted you," he muttered, as he sat down, his hand immediately going to her forehead, checking for a fever.

She smiled, her whole face wrinkling up in delight at his action. "I only came from the clinic," she stated, "just a few feet away."

"I know, and you're already beat. What the hell made you think you would be safe here?"

"Of all the places somebody would choose to make trouble," she explained, "I figured this would be at the bottom of the list."

"How the hell did you know it was my place anyway?" he asked. The relief he felt when he realized she was okay was immense. That she'd chosen to come to his place warmed his heart, but still he wanted to rail at her for being so stupid.

Yet he knew what it was like, when you felt that instinct to bolt. When something was going so wrong in your world, and it seemed you had absolutely no choice, sometimes that need to run was overwhelming, and you could do nothing but give in to it. He settled down, unable to help himself, as he gathered her up gently and pulled her into his arms.

She didn't argue. Instead she curled up and rested.

"Even getting dressed must have hurt like hell."

"It was better than I thought," she replied, against his

chest, "but Sydney was a help."

"Of course she was, and she's also pretty worried. Worried sick actually. Especially when she didn't seem to know where you were going."

Amelia smiled. "I knew you would figure it out."

"I almost didn't," he admitted.

"Yeah, but you did, so *almost didn't* doesn't work for me."

As that was something Mountain's own father would have said, and his grandfather too, over the years, Mountain held her close.

"It was the voice," she added, "that taunting voice. That's the thing that got me."

"Yeah, and I have a pretty good idea whose taunting voice that is," he shared. "You just may not have heard it used in that way."

"I'm torn between two possibilities."

"I wasn't even thinking we had two. I was pretty sure it would be the one." When she told him her guess of the two names, he nodded.

"I'm surprised at the one, … but, ever since you mentioned Joe and what he went through and his family connection to Elijah, that makes sense in a way," Mountain noted.

"You really think it could be anybody else?"

"I'm pretty sure it is somebody else," he murmured. "The problem has been trying to prove it. In a case like this, you can't accuse somebody of these types of crimes and expect to walk away from it or have anybody believe you. So it's absolutely imperative that we get the proof so we can put a stop to it."

"You don't think you can do anything to put a stop to it

yourself?" she asked bluntly.

"Oh, absolutely," he replied, his tone equally blunt. "A bullet would do it." When she winced, he nodded. "As much as I've been tempted to drop this asshole, I still have doubts, and therefore …" Then his voice fell away.

"And therefore," she added, "you can't shoot him because it's the wrong thing to do."

He smiled and gently kissed her forehead. "As much as I'm glad that you knew where to come to be safe, I still wish you were back in the clinic, so I would know you are safe in a medical sense."

She snorted at that. "No, you don't wish I was back there. You're happy I'm here." She got another squeeze for that, as he admitted she was right.

"Maybe, but the timing could be better."

"I don't think timing has anything to do with it," she muttered. "I don't trust easily, and neither do you."

"No, I sure don't," he admitted, with a sigh. "Yet you earned my trust, by keeping my brother alive."

She tilted her head back, looked up at him, and smiled. "And I didn't even know I was being tested," she teased.

"You weren't. … You were absolutely not being tested in any way," he replied, "but still, that's the good news because you came through with flying colors regardless."

"How would you feel about …"

He looked down at her and immediately shook his head.

She glared at him. "You don't know me well enough to know what I'm thinking," she snapped.

"And, if you didn't think I knew you that well," he argued, tapping her nose gently, "you … wouldn't … have … come … here. And, no, I won't use you as bait."

Her shoulders sagged against him, and he cuddled her

close. He didn't know what the hell was happening, but it was obvious to both of them that something was here, something precious, something he did not want to take any chances with.

"We have to do something," she muttered in exasperation.

"Maybe, but that doesn't mean it has to be using you as bait."

"So, use somebody else then," she suggested immediately. "Somebody my height, somebody capable of looking like me." She pulled back to look at him, and his lips twitched. "I can't keep living in fear. Either I give him an opportunity to take me out or I ensure that I'm a long way away. I'm not even sure why I'm a target to begin with."

"Because whoever was lining up for a shot that day is somebody you saw."

"Right, I remember that," she murmured. "Yet I didn't think I *saw him*-saw him."

"You did presumably, or he thinks you did. Or ..." Mountain hesitated. "Or he's just an asshole, and you're on his list, and, for whatever reason, you made that list, and now he's bound and determined to put a checkmark by your name going forward." She shook her head at the thought, but he nodded. "You know I'm right." At that, she glared at him, and he chuckled. "See? There are two sides to this *reading your mind* thing."

"Yeah, I'm seeing that," she muttered. "Doesn't mean I like it though."

"Of course not. There's an openness, a naked vulnerability in knowing that you can know my thoughts and understand who I am and what I'm saying, without saying it," he shared. "Can't say it's particularly comfortable on my end either, but it doesn't change the fact that we're both here in this situation, whether we like it or not."

"We can always walk away," she suggested.

"We could," he noted, "but I won't, and neither will you."

Her lips twitched. "I'm not even sure what *this* is," she admitted, with an eye roll.

"No, and that's why we have to figure out the rest of this mess, to then focus on us," he shared, with more cheerfulness than he felt. As he pondered her idea further, he nodded. "I think you're right. Somehow though, it has to look like it's you, and it has to appear that you're sneaking out because this asshole will know quite well who is involved with you."

"Because he's always there, watching, like Joe."

"And yet I'm pretty sure it isn't Joe," he admitted.

She winced. "I would hate to think that anybody who loves dogs the way I do would be capable of this."

"The thing is, … this mess isn't about dogs, although two were injured when someone shot at Magnus early on. The thing is, while Joe does love dogs, a part of him … absolutely despises people."

"Yeah, I know," she said, "but we already think we know who the real killer is. We know who we're being pointed at, but that doesn't mean it's the same thing as finding the right man." She sighed, resting against Mountain.

He nodded. She was too tired; he could tell that from the way she was acting. "I sure as hell wish you were a long way from here."

"Me too," she murmured. "I wish I hadn't come in the first place."

"Not me. I won't go that far," he replied, with a gentle smile, as he cuddled her close. "I've been looking for you practically since I got here." When she twisted and looked up at him, he nodded. "You know I was. I just didn't know why. Obviously I was trying to get answers and to find my brother, but there's so much more to it than that."

"Instincts," she suggested, "finding that part of you, finding that piece of your soul that's been missing and that you didn't even know about." And then she laughed. "It sounds like so much garbage."

"That's because both of us have been hurt, and, in some ways, we've isolated ourselves," he admitted. "I wasn't even sure if you would see the attraction between us."

"Seeing is one thing," she noted, with a smile, "but doing something about it? Now that's a completely different issue."

He burst out laughing. "But you already made that choice, and that's why you're here."

She shrugged. "Maybe. I also figured that nobody in their right mind would cross you." His laughter boomed, and she held a finger up against his lips. "Is It safe?" she asked in a low tone. "Or will somebody assume that I'm here?"

"I don't know whether they will or not," he said, squeezing her as much as he could without hurting her, "because, right about now, everything will blow wide open."

"Maybe, but that doesn't mean we're up to that point."

Just then came a distinctive knock on the door. He called out, "Come in."

Samson stepped inside.

Mountain eyed him and nodded. "I can see you had the same reaction I did to what Elijah had to say."

"It's … I don't want to say farfetched, but it's damn frustrating."

"Yeah, I know, and is Chef stringing us a line, telling us a story, still protecting a friend—or his son?"

"That's the thing, ... *or his son.*"

She looked from one to the other. "Whoa, wait, but he said, ... didn't someone say Chef's son was dead?"

Mountain looked down at her. "His son isn't dead after all, as far as we know, or so we've been told. His son is alive and still in the military but under a completely different name. In order to keep the son safe, he changed his name and took on somebody else's name," Mountain explained. "And the results of that was that we have somebody buried under a wrong name, being impersonated by somebody else."

"But who the hell is it?" she asked, looking at him in surprise. Her gaze went from one man to the other.

"What do you think?" Mountain asked Samson.

Samson shook his head. "I think it could be either one, except there's another horrible possibility in the back of my head too."

"That they're all in on it?"

"And yet that doesn't make sense either," Samson admitted. "And I can't imagine how—in any way, shape, or form—that would make sense to Elijah."

"And yet how does any of this make sense to anybody?" Mountain asked Samson. When another knock came on his door again, Mountain groaned. "Since when did my room become Grand Central Station?"

"Since you decided to hide in here, ... with our damsel in distress," Samson pointed out, with half a smile in Amelia's direction.

Amelia looked at him, surprised, and then nodded. "I guess that makes sense, but maybe I should have stayed in the clinic."

"Then why didn't you?" Samson looked at her intently.

She hesitated, then replied, "If I said *instincts*, would that make sense to you?"

He shrugged. "As much as anything here does. Yes."

"It could also have been overwhelming fear," she admitted. "The killer's comments were meant to send me off, but I didn't want it to be permanent."

Samson went to the door and walked back into the room again with Magnus, as the two of them looked at Mountain and frowned. Mountain nodded. "I understand. We need a meeting, but Amelia has an idea that I'm fighting against. The trouble is, it has merit."

"Setting her up as bait?" Samson asked immediately.

She looked over at him from the comfort of Mountain's arms and nodded. "It's not a bad idea, is it?"

"I won't say it's the right idea," he replied. "Nobody wants to see you get hurt again, and you're taking a hell of a chance."

"Sure, we all are," she admitted. "So am I, but I'm in danger already. I still don't understand why I would be a target, but I do understand that I am one. I'll worry about the why after we're all safe."

Samson gave her a nod of approval. "That's a good way to look at it, but let's not take any chances right now."

"But … you want to tell them?" Mountain asked her.

Amelia nodded. "My thought was that somebody could pretend to be me, and you guys could use them as the bait."

Samson immediately nodded again. "Barret has already volunteered."

She looked at him in surprise, contemplated it, and asked, "He's not my body type, is he?"

"He is not. He's a bit on the bigger side, but the height is more or less the same. From a distance, nobody will really know, and, if we give him some of your clothing, we'll have a better chance at pulling this off. We already tested it out, and he can fit into your parka."

She looked at him in surprise and then nodded. "Honestly, that's probably all that would be required."

"We would hope so, but there's no guarantee," he said cautiously. "However, taking this directly to you, the way the killer did, he's almost issued a challenge, so I suggest we meet it and break it."

I T WAS AN odd thing to think of somebody else going out as a sacrificial lamb for her. Amelia mentioned it several times to Barret, who gently smiled and tapped her on the cheek. "You did your part. Let us do ours."

"I feel as if you've already done so much," she murmured.

Nikolai stepped up beside her. "Barret won't be out there alone. I'll go too, and others, and we've got a sled and will be taking your dogs," he shared, with a nod. "I need to be part of this, and I'm pretty sure that this … I won't say it all started with my father, but it certainly involves my father."

She winced and nodded. "Got it," she murmured. "Good luck, you guys. I'll stay here and hope that it all happens way the hell out there." Then she hesitated. "What about …" She winced. "What about Elijah's son?"

"Yeah, that's another problem because we don't know who we'll come up against in the wilderness," Nikolai shared. "As long as he's not here with you, then chances are we're okay."

"Maybe," Amelia replied. "We also don't know for sure that somebody else isn't involved."

Samson placed a hand on her shoulder. "And we're prepared for that too. Now I need you to go back to your room and wait." She hesitated, but Mountain gave her a look. She glared at him. "I won't always be so agreeable," she announced.

His grin flashed. "Is this being agreeable? I can't imagine what you *not being agreeable* will look like."

"You're about to find out," she declared, with a threatening note in her tone.

Mountain leaned over, picked her up with absolutely no effort, and gave her a bruising kiss. When he put her down, he whispered, "Now hang on to that thought, until we get back."

And, with that, they snuck out in staggered groups. She slowly made her way back to his room, wishing she had brought coffee or something with her to help make it a little easier to wait. When a knock came on the door, and Sydney's soft voice identified herself, Amelia opened the door to find Sydney with a tray of food and drink. Amelia looked at her in surprise and relief. "How did you know I was sitting here, wishing I had thought to bring something?"

"Considering that we're still not letting you move around very much, you've already done more than you should have," the doc said in a scolding tone.

Amelia sat back down on the bed, with the tray of goodies in front of her, and looked at Sydney. "Will you join me?"

Sydney nodded. "That was the plan. You'll find other people will be coming by too, as we are all taking shifts."

She stopped and looked at her carefully. "Meaning, I'm not allowed to be alone, *huh*?"

The doc gave her a cheeky grin. "What do you think? Yeah, not happening," Sydney declared. "Mountain has done an awful lot to help everybody here, so we'll all do an awful lot to help him."

"And not me?" Amelia teased, with an eye roll.

"And you," Sydney confirmed, with that same cheerfulness. "We want to ensure this comes to an end."

"Me too," Amelia muttered. "I want to know that, whatever I do from here on out, I can do without looking behind me all the time."

"That's the worst, isn't it?" Sydney noted, her voice quiet. "We went through some tough times here before—I won't even say, *before this all blew up*, since it was certainly in the process of blowing up. We just didn't know it yet," she explained. "Anyway it wasn't fun for any of us, so I do understand what you're going through to a certain extent."

Amelia studied Sydney and realized she really did understand, and empathy had filled her gaze too. "You must be good at your job," Amelia noted in a quiet voice.

Sydney looked at her in surprise and laughed. "I don't know about that, but I do my best to help. Sometimes you can't do what you need to do, and that's heartbreaking, and sometimes, for all your efforts, it still won't be enough, and that's definitely heartbreaking too."

"Surely some good is in it."

"Yes, … absolutely there is. Sometimes there are miracles. Those are breathtaking too, and I absolutely love every minute of every day when that becomes a possibility," she shared with a bright, cheerful smile. "The day that Teegan turned up, that was a miracle we all needed." Sydney gave Amelia a clipped nod. "A miracle made possible by you. Mountain was absolutely devastated that his brother had gone missing for so long, and all the more frustrated when he couldn't find him. And, because of his brother, Mountain's the one who sounded the alarm up here. Because of everything he mobilized, this operation is ongoing right now."

"So now it just needs to come to a conclusion."

"Exactly, and that conclusion needs to be the right one," the doc noted, "and hopefully before we lose anyone else."

"And yet somehow I suspect that, before this is over, maybe even before this night is over," Amelia said, "we could have more dead than anticipated." Sydney looked at her, startled, and Amelia shrugged. "I think, when they've cornered this rat, it'll become beyond dangerous, and it won't be easy on anybody involved."

Sydney nodded. "I won't argue with you on that. ... I hope it doesn't cost us any of those people who are out there doing so much to keep the rest of us safe."

Amelia realized Magnus was out there too. "Oh, God. I'm sorry, Sydney. I shouldn't have brought it up." But she got a headshake in return.

"I don't live in a world of denial," Sydney replied. "Absolutely no point, not up here. I'm perfectly aware of what people can be like and how rough this world can be. ... So we'll stay strong, wait and hope for the best."

They huddled up, and they talked for a while about nothing and yet everything, as they tried to forget about what was going on around them. Later, when a knock came on the door, and Sandrine poked her head in, Sydney got up with a smile and ushered her in.

"My turn to man the clinic," Sydney explained to Amelia. "You take care now." And, with that, she was gone.

Sandrine bounced in and sat down in front of Amelia. "Hey. How are you holding up?"

"I was doing pretty well, until I realized how many were outside and how the rest have to babysit me."

"Either that or you're back in the clinic," she pointed

out. "Which would you prefer?"

"Here," Amelia said immediately, and then she chuckled. "What a question."

"Right?" Sandrine said, with a bright, cheerful smile. "Just think. So much is going on right now, and the base is abuzz. Nobody really knows what's happening, but they all know something's happening."

"You'd have to be dead not to," Amelia noted, with a headshake. "Everybody here is pretty damn smart."

"They are, aren't they? It's been amazing to see how people here interact with each other. I came here very recently, so I wasn't a part of any of the original mess and found myself in an odd scenario where I didn't really fit in with anyone. For a while it was pretty wild, but I ended up spending most of my time with Teegan anyway. Of course Teegan and I have a history."

"Maybe you should tell me about that history," Amelia suggested, with a smile, "because he did mention your name a time or two."

Sandrine stared at her in shock.

Amelia nodded. "When I tried to question him on it, he went silent."

"No need to be alarmed, but I would guess it was mostly because he didn't remember *us* anymore," Sandrine suggested, with a laugh. Then she explained their history and soon had both of them laughing.

"Oh, gosh, the things that we get ourselves into, and then we don't know how to fix it," Amelia noted, with a laugh. "And I'm not even sure where or how I got into this, but apparently I'm somewhat involved with Mountain."

"Oh, well, if you have to pick somebody to get involved with here," Sandrine said, "you picked a good one. That man is all heart. According to what I've heard from everybody else, he didn't leave a stone unturned, trying to find his brother. He was pretty damn sure that you had him, but he wasn't convinced enough that he could rest about it. Yet he never could catch up with you. Then, when you brought in Teegan, Mountain just knew it had been you. He was desperate to talk to you and to see if you had answers. He spent days out there looking for you, once Teegan showed up here."

"I know," she muttered. "I saw him out there, but I wasn't sure of his motives or what he was doing. I didn't know he was Teegan's brother at that point. I would watch him from a distance," Amelia admitted, "unsure about what to do. Teegan had been so emphatic about not trusting anybody here at the base, so I didn't feel comfortable calling out to Mountain and letting him know where I was. Plus, I've heard since then how Mountain didn't show up here until after Teegan had been missing for about three weeks. So it's not like Teegan knew his brother was here, although he was praying for him to get here."

"And that just made it all that much harder on Mountain," Sandrine stated, with a nod. "On the other hand, Mountain should have to work for it," she teased, followed by a chuckle.

Amelia rolled her eyes at that. "I don't know about *work for it*, but I think Mountain would do anything to keep his brother alive."

"Almost as much as you did," Sandrine noted, with a pointed look. "I can't imagine all that you went through to do that, dealing with the fear of wondering who could be trusted or if you could trust anybody at all."

"That was the problem, not knowing who was trustworthy, and knowing that, as far as Teegan was concerned, I couldn't trust anybody in this base. So, I didn't dare take this poor man and put him back into the same scenario that he'd barely survived in the first place," she murmured. "And yet I didn't have anybody to ask, to talk to, to help me work my way through it."

"You got here in the end."

"Only because I was shot again. If I'd known Mountain, as I do now, it would have been a different story," she admitted, with a shrug, "but, even still, I'm going on instincts, trusting him at this point."

"And so you should," Sandrine said. "That's the one person you can trust."

There was something comforting about hearing that, and it confirmed what Amelia already knew, but it helped. It shouldn't have helped, but it did, and, for that, she was grateful to have yet another little nudge of confirmation.

When they finished their leftover food and tea, Amelia asked, almost in desperation, "So, how long do you get to stay here?"

"Oh, don't worry. You'll get a steady stream of people," she replied. "I am damn sure you won't be alone."

"I won't argue with that," Amelia muttered.

"It seems as if we're all very heavily involved in keeping people alive here," Sandrine noted, with a quick nod. "Too many people, too many things going wrong."

"Got it." Amelia nodded. "I'm worried about the men out there and now I'm worried about my dogs being out there too, part of the con, so I don't even have them for comfort."

"I understand. I think Joe wanted to come over and see you too, so maybe that'll be part of your visitation today."

"I'd be okay with that," she said, with a bright smile. "I do like him."

"We all do. He's a sweetheart, and he's just looking to go home at the end of this training session and have time with his wife." She jumped to her feet and announced, "Okay, my time's up. I'll check to see if your next replacement is there."

With that comment, she stepped out, closing the door immediately and leaving Amelia to question what she'd just heard.

MOUNTAIN HAD DOUBTS if this would work, but they had to try. As he drove the snowcat up to the scientist's camp, he looked over at Magnus. "I can't imagine that, in this weather, he would even be bothered."

"I can't imagine in this weather that he can afford *not* to be bothered," Magnus stated immediately.

Mountain frowned at that and grudgingly nodded. "I suppose it's possible."

Magnus smiled, trying to keep it light. "We have to give it a try, and we both know it."

"Oh, I agree, and that's why we're here." They parked at the scientists' camp. Then the two of them got out and immediately geared up to now be directly in the weather and walked back to the military base, keeping to the rises. They were dressed in all whiteout gear, as they deliberately hid their tracks, keeping their own visibility to a minimum, yet with the best view for themselves as they possibly could.

Using hand signals as they walked because noise traveled terribly far in this weather, they moved swiftly, until they saw Barret coming toward them, moving at a steady pace.

He was struggling a little bit with the sled, and the four dogs, but then that would also look a whole lot better and more accurate to anyone assuming he was Amelia. He was also geared up with a bulletproof vest, just in case, and he had a special helmet on underneath Amelia's heavy parka. Anything for added protection, considering he was bait.

As Magnus and Mountain stayed up in the hills, they eventually crouched down and checked to see if there was any sign of anyone else. This was the dicey part because they must see their adversary, before they were seen themselves.

Barret had Amelia's dogs, the four of them, and they had decent-enough training and experience that the dogs were willing to go with him. Barret headed up to the scientists' camp, where they decided Amelia would most likely go in order to keep herself safe, particularly after saying that she'd been there time and time again, staying until she felt it was too dangerous and leaving again.

Barret moved steadily, using shoulder strokes to match Amelia's height, crouched over slightly to one side, as Amelia would be favoring her injured side, from where she'd been shot. They watched decoy Barret going slow and steady, noting his faltering progress.

Beside Mountain, Magnus whispered, "Damn, I hope he's faking it, and, if he is, he's doing a hell of a job. If he's not faking it, I would say he's in trouble."

"I know. I was thinking the same thing," Mountain murmured, as they remained here on this western edge, crouched down. Off in the distance, coming around on the eastern side, would be Nikolai. No way he would stay on the sidelines and out of this scenario. Egan and Rogan were at opposite ends of the tundra, and all the good guys out here had long guns on them.

Elijah was on lockdown at the base, with Samson keeping a close eye on him, along with Whalen and Teegan as backup, just to ensure Chef wouldn't go anywhere.

Mountain had filled in Magnus on everything they had heard from Elijah yesterday, and, not surprisingly, both of them were still processing the newest information.

Magnus muttered, "I can't believe that the three of them are so intertwined."

"Nobody really knew," Mountain murmured. "But that's the thing, right? Nobody knew, and, because nobody knew, they could get away with all kinds of stuff, and yet who's getting away with what?"

"That's the problem," Magnus noted, as he looked over—checking to the north, where Egan should be—deliberately making his movements slow and steady, so nobody else would pick up on him being there. He then checked to the south for Rogan. "I don't see anything out there," Magnus noted, his voice soft.

Mountain replied, "No, not yet, but that doesn't mean jack shit though, and you know that." They stayed hunkered down for another fifteen minutes, and just as he was about to believe that this was a no-go, a shot rang out. He watched in horror as Barret stumbled and slowly slid to the ground.

"Shit." Magnus immediately tried to bolt to his feet, but Mountain held him down.

"Hold up," he said, warning him in a low hiss. "If he's down, we'll get him, but, if he's faking it, we can't give him up. We have to catch whoever's doing this, or it's all for nothing."

Magnus struggled against the restraint, but, when Mountain was sure Magnus wouldn't break their cover, the big man shifted ever-so-slightly. Mountain whispered,

"Remember. Every movement and every sound up here is amplified."

"Sure, but so is the wind, the air, everything," Magnus muttered in frustration. "This place is deadly, without anybody trying to take us out. With people *trying* to take us out, it's beyond deadly."

"Exactly, and that's part of the problem," Mountain said. "We can't allow anybody else to play this game."

"And yet how the hell did our lives become a game? They shouldn't be. They should never have become a part of it," Magnus muttered.

"But you and I both know that they did, so something is completely messed up here." Mountain watched and waited, relieved when he saw Barret give a small hand signal, which they had decided upon beforehand. "He's fine," he said, then sighed. "Not *fine* necessarily, but he's given us a signal that he's okay."

"Good enough," Magnus replied at his side, his breathing calming down. "Damn it."

"I know. Believe me. I know," he said, at his side, "I don't want anything to happen to him either—or to anybody else."

"Who's on Amelia?"

"All the women are taking shifts, plus Joe."

"Who's on Elijah?" Magnus asked.

"Samson and Whalen and Teegan. Hopefully we won't be too long out here that we need a second shift for Elijah." Mountain looked at Magnus from the corner of his eye. "Do you think we need another shift?"

"I just … don't know. We don't know how many people are involved in this shit." Magnus groaned. "I can't imagine that all this time Elijah managed to keep anybody in control."

"The trouble is, this is the first base assignment where both Joe and Elijah were with him," Mountain pointed out, "and that's part of the problem."

"It's not only part of the problem, as it's apparently blown the lid off everything."

"Exactly, and that's why it's such a problem. Seems somebody started to lose control over our killer, and what wasn't an issue before is a huge issue now."

"Christ," Magnus muttered, as they sat here and watched. "How long will we wait?"

"I'm not sure," Mountain answered in a monotone. "As long as we have to. We're looking for any sign of anybody out there. Remember. When he shot Amelia, he checked on her and told her *Good riddance*. Plus he tormented her in the clinic, with more threatening words. He likes to confront his victims." All of a sudden, Mountain saw it. "Wait. Nine o'clock. Moving slowly,"

Magnus shifted enough that he could see. "Oh, that little bastard," he muttered.

"Yeah, and the question is, is Nikolai the closest?"

"That is one issue, but our second one is, are we sure our nine o'clock target is *not* Nikolai?" Magnus asked, with a note of humor.

"Yeah, we're absolutely sure our nine o'clock is *not* Nikolai," Mountain noted, with a frustrated tone. "But, if anybody had reasons to ensure this went down the way we all want it to, believe me, it's Nikolai. He's avenging his father's killer."

"How the fuck are you so calm right now?" Magnus muttered. "Do you think … Will Barret lose it?"

"No, he won't," Mountain stated, his voice firm. "He's a

good man, and he knows what's at stake."

"I know he knows what's at stake, but that doesn't mean that, when it comes down to it, anybody'll have any control. This could potentially go south and very, very quickly."

As they watched, Barret shifted ever-so-slightly, enough that they knew he was alive and okay, but not necessarily enough that he knew he was about to be attacked. The wait had to be deadly for Barret, expecting to be ambushed and unable to see it coming.

As Mountain sat here, lining up a shot himself, as the others did so too, the target figure, moving ever-so-slowly on skis, neared Barret. Amid the complete whiteout, the wind picked up, and the storm around them started to scream its own hell and fury. Mountain groaned softly.

"What is it about Mother Nature," Magnus murmured at his side, "that makes her such a bitch."

"I think she's pissed that we're disturbing her peace and quiet," Mountain suggested. "You've got to think that she didn't bring this on. This is all man-made, this problem, and she doesn't take kindly to this evil interference in her world."

"And yet she doesn't really care," Magnus noted, smiling. "If you think about it, she's waiting for the dust to settle, so that her clean-up crew can come in and pick the flesh off our bones."

"Nice way to put it," Mountain muttered, yet with a smile. "Still, I would rather have a polar bear take me down, than some two-legged asshole."

"I won't argue with you there," Magnus replied, as they watched the figure slowly line up closer and closer to Barret. "I sure hope Barret's ready for this."

"You and me both," Mountain murmured. "Not only that, I think the other three guys are moving around.

Nikolai's out there, but he's not alone now. I can see him, but somebody's with him."

"So either Egan or Rogan," Magnus muttered.

"Yep. Either way, Nikolai's in good hands."

"Are you sure about Samson? He's an unknown entity in all this. I haven't quite figured out that guy. Something is off about him."

Mountain chuckled. "In some ways there is. As soon as you figure it out, you'll be kicking yourself."

Magnus stared at him keenly, trying to make sense of what he said, when a shot rang out, followed by dead silence.

DAY 7 AFTERNOON

A S FAR AS Amelia was concerned, this waiting was unbearable. The women had been playing cards, switching up people, having tea or coffee, and still there was no news. Nobody revealed their nervousness, but Amelia couldn't get over the feeling that something was seriously wrong.

When the switch of her guard came again, she groaned and turned to look at the present company. "Somebody needs to go out there and confirm those guys are okay."

Sydney eyed her carefully. "Nobody is more capable of being out there than those guys."

Amelia swallowed and nodded. "I could go."

"You could go, but do what?" Sydney asked curiously. "It's not as if we can communicate with them. It's not as if we can tell them that you're out there or to watch out because you decided to go play hero," the doc pointed out. "It's not as if we can warn them, so they don't accidentally shoot you," she added, with a raised eyebrow.

Just enough logic had been presented by Sydney to totally piss off Amelia, yet she understood. "I still think something's wrong," she muttered, "and surely there's got to be some way to make it right." Then the door opened yet again, and she looked up to see Joe, a big grin on his face.

He looked over at Sydney. "Hey, I begged for this

chance. I can stay with her, so you can go off and grab yourself a cup of coffee."

Sydney laughed. "Okay, I'm good with that." She looked back at Amelia. "Do you want something to eat?"

She winced at that. "As much as I don't really want to, I probably should."

"Yes, you probably should." And, with that, Sydney got up. "Let me go see if there are any groceries to be had." And. with that, she headed out.

As soon as she was gone, Amelia looked over at Joe. "Have you heard anything?"

He shook his head. "No, I haven't, but I'm not sure what's going on either," he admitted, "so you probably shouldn't ask me questions about it because I don't know anything. I've purposely kept to myself in the dog barn. I didn't want anything to do with the mess at this base."

"Right." She nodded. "It's all so frustrating."

"Of course it is, but you also have to trust in these men."

"I trust them. I'm just not sure I trust the asshole out there trying to ruin them."

He looked at her in surprise. "It seems I'm not privy to any current information."

She backed off at that and nodded lightly. "I am a little confused, though, about something else. Sandrine mentioned that you want to spend some time with your wife, but I thought your wife had passed away."

He looked at her for a long moment. "When did you hear that?"

She frowned and then thought about it. "I'm not exactly sure to be honest, but it was mentioned casually that you were looking forward to going back to spending time with her, and that surprised me because I'd understood that your wife was already gone. Of course that's a terrible thing to ask you about, and I'm sorry for that."

He shrugged. "Lots of people in my world are gone," he replied, with an odd smile, "and sometimes I think I'm better off if I go with them."

"Oh, that's not a good topic either."

He burst out laughing and nodded. "No, it probably isn't, but I don't have any secrets."

She looked at him carefully from the corner of her eye. "Don't you?"

Surprised, he stared at her for a long moment. "Aren't you a clever one."

"Not sure that *clever* is quite the right word," she replied, hating the direction her thoughts were going. "But what are the chances that they left me here, while they're out there trying to find the asshole who's killing people, and you're here right in front of me?"

He stared at her for a long moment, but she could glean absolutely nothing from the look in his eyes. He gave her a bright smile and chuckled lightly. "You're partially right. … I'm not killing anybody here, but neither have I done anything to stop it."

"The problem is, I don't understand any of this, so why don't we sit here, and you tell me what the hell's going on? At least the part that you do know."

He stared off in the distance and shrugged. "Not sure that's a good idea," he murmured.

"And yet, why not?" she asked. "You know it needs to end." His laugh, when it came, was half broken, and so much pain was attached to it that she didn't know how to help him.

He sat back, looked at her, and then slowly nodded. "It

is probably time, and, of everybody, you deserve to know."

She let out a slow, deep breath, still not exactly sure what she'd triggered here. "So, tell me."

In a quiet voice, he sat back in his chair and stared off in the distance. "We'd been married many years," he began, "at least thirty-two. My wife was forever berating me because I could never quite remember the exact number," he said, with a soft smile.

"I think men all over the world have that problem," Amelia stated, with a gentle laugh.

"Yeah, and I was no different. We had a baby boy, the absolute love of our lives, the best thing to ever happen to us. He was …" He stopped for a moment and smiled. "He was perfect."

She smiled up at him. "That's how every parent should consider their child," she noted.

"We had such fun with him. We spent so much time up here in the north, my wife too, because she loved it as well. We spent all of our holidays with the dogs out in the snow, camping in ice caves, and generally loving everything about it. And, when he grew up, … he wanted to go into the military. I wasn't so sure. I'd done my stint, and I'd done a ton of contracts for them. Some of them were fine, but it was an admirable thing for him, and his heart was set on it, so there wasn't a whole lot that would dissuade him," Joe shared, with half a smile. "Of course you never know the next moment from this one." He fell silent for a long time.

"You've never mentioned him before," she stated. "What became of him?"

He looked at her with an odd smile. "He disappeared, went MIA, and we didn't have any answers forever. As a matter of fact, … we have no idea what happened to this day. I don't think there's any news that's worse than having no news," he shared. "You're forever waiting for that letter that tells you that he's on his way home or that phone call that says, *Surprise, he's at the airport*, but we never got any word. Not even the proverbial military-uniformed man confirming the death of our son. It broke my wife. She lasted a few more years, and then she finally gave up the hope of his return, … devastated and heartbroken. We only ever had the one child, you see? So, when you only have one, that child becomes everything. When he passed or disappeared," he said, "we had nothing left to go on, except hope."

"So, you kept going then, even after her passing?"

"I did. I kept hoping. I kept doing military contracts. I kept looking for him, hoping I would see his face, hoping I would see him out in the middle of somewhere, that he would be here, that he would be smiling and happy. Maybe he had a concussion. Maybe he had amnesia. Maybe he had all kinds of things," Joe suggested, "but there was always that hope that he was alive somewhere. After my wife died, I knew that the chance of getting answers was getting slimmer and slimmer. I had desperately wanted to get the one answer that would help me out, but it wasn't to be. She died without ever knowing what happened to him."

"So, both you and Elijah lost your sons," she said, with a nod.

He gave her a strange look. "Elijah was married to my wife's sister, and she died many years earlier. Breast cancer. I don't even remember when," he said, with an awkward laugh. "Honestly, we were dealing with our own heartaches and problems of another sort at that point in time." He gave a wave of his hand. "I don't even remember what it was. I think it was my in-laws passing."

Joe shook his head. "Anyway, yes, Elijah lost his son," Joe confirmed, with quiet emphasis, "and he stayed in and became a lifer. I think maybe partly because of that I did too. Obviously I'm not full military, but I do constant contracts with them," he noted. "And still, in the back of my mind, was this opportunity to see my son somewhere. Even if only to find his body lost somewhere, but it wasn't to be."

She watched him, as he tried to swallow the tears and not let them roll.

"It wasn't to be," he repeated. "And then I was here on this base, during this particular training session, and I was doing my usual thing with the dogs. One of the men, the day sergeant, came over," Joe said, with a smile. "We talked for a few minutes, and I found out his name was Chester. That was my son's name too. I was friendly. … When here for a survival training session, I try to be friendly to these guys, yet I like my solitude. Still, some of these guys don't have much for families, and some of these guys leave families behind. Sometimes you can have a distant relationship with some of them. As I got to talking with him, … he mentioned something that surprised me, and I didn't say more about it for a while, but then I asked him about it later. And he looked at me and lied point-blank to my face. *I don't know what you're talking about,* he said to me. *I'm not sure what drink you've been drinking, but I didn't mention anything like that.* He seemed so honest and sincere that I thought, well, maybe I didn't quite understand what he had said. However, his words wouldn't leave me alone."

"What was it that he said?"

"Doesn't matter, but finally, when I had an opportunity, and I had to be sneaky about that opportunity," Joe shared, with a nod, "I checked his full name, only to find that it was a play on words of my son's name. That hit me hard, you know? I mean, I'm sure people all over the world share an exact name with someone across the globe. Still, the similarities were hard to ignore. My son was Chester Fibke." Joe sighed. "This other guy, the day sergeant, was Chester Fibek, like the last name had been misspelled."

"That could be some mistake or coincidence, right?"

"Close, but not close enough. I don't know. I was so surprised by it. I didn't think anything of it at first, but it kept nagging and nagging at me, and finally it took a bit of time and some money to find out that his real name had been changed from Chester Fibke to Chester Fibek," he said, his voice breaking.

She stared at him for a long moment, not comprehending. "Sorry?"

He nodded. "Yeah, I'm not surprised that you're confused," he replied. "Believe me, I was too."

She didn't quite get it, but her mind was working its way through it. "So, your son changed his name?" she asked cautiously.

He shook his head. "No, my son didn't change his name because the man who had been using my son's name was not my son."

MOUNTAIN AND MAGNUS raced toward the convergence of the two men, as several other shots rang out, but luckily the bullets weren't coming in their direction, or so it seemed. Out here, sounds were distorted. So just because gunshots didn't appear to be headed to you, they still could be. It added to the dangers up here. By the time they reached

Barret, he was staring up at the sky above him, blinking hard.

"Did you take a hit?" Mountain asked Barret immediately, as the big man ducked down beside him. Magnus was right there with them, weapons ready, as he fired several warning shots.

Barret looked up at Mountain. "Yeah, I took a couple hits," he murmured, "but I think they're in my vest. I don't think they went through. Honest to God, I'm lying here trying to catch my breath," he admitted, with a constricted laugh. "It seemed the simplest thing to do."

"Yeah, you're not kidding," Mountain muttered, as relief washed over him when he checked out Barret. Then shout-outs came. He answered them, with the news of another one down. That left them with a total of two they had shot down, and quickly they were surrounded by Nikolai's and Rogan's and Egan's voices, all overlapping.

"Damn it, speak one at a time," Mountain snapped.

"We have another man down off to the side," Nikolai said.

Mountain nodded. "Dead?"

"Soon to be dead."

"Do we know who he is?"

"Yeah, we know who he is. At least one of the two. The other one? ... Well, he's our mystery participant in this mess," Egan shared, as he looked down at Barret. "How are you doing, buddy?"

"I'm okay," he replied, with a smile. "I'm just not too anxious to move. I think I took one in the chest and one in the shoulder."

"Let's hope the bulletproof vest held you in good stead."

"I think it did, but it still hurts to take a hit. I don't

want to move just yet," he said, with a snort.

They all looked in the direction of the second man.

"I'm still confused," Magnus said, staring at the nearest body. "This is the colonel, and over there is the day sergeant. How the hell are they connected?"

"He's the other partner we weren't sure about," Mountain explained, as he frowned at the injured colonel. Mountain would love to leave him to die in the cold but … "Now we need to get everybody back to the base and fast. This one is shot up pretty bad, but let's see if we can get any answers out of him before he dies on us."

"Both are pretty shot up," Nikolai confirmed, as he checked the second downed man. "As far as I'm concerned, he could rot up here, but we don't know if he's dead yet, do we? And, if he's alive, we need answers."

With that, Rogan and Egan ran to get the snowcat, while the rest of the men split up to carry the injured. Mountain walked over to the colonel, on his back in the snow, staring up at the sky. When Mountain crouched beside him, the colonel rolled his head to the side and looked at him, giving a gurgled laugh. "I figured you would get me."

"Yeah, we got you. I sure wish I understood why though," Mountain replied, as he lifted the colonel.

"Elijah can explain," he murmured. "If not, I'm pretty damn sure Joe would tell you all about it." Then he gave a heavy breath and died in Mountain's arms.

Mountain slowly straightened up, carrying the body, then called out to the others, "The colonel's gone, but he did say that Elijah and Joe could tell us what this is all about."

"Let's get everybody back to base then because this guy's still alive," Nikolai said, crouching over Chester to get his pulse.

Magnus was near Barret, telling him to rest until the snowcat arrived. "Guys, some of you will be on skis getting back to base, so we have room for three to be prone inside the cat, but let's all stick together."

Nikolai drove the snowcat, with Chester, Barret, and the colonel quickly loaded inside. Mountain handed out the skis from the snowcat to the others. With Egan bringing the sled and the dogs, Mountain, Magnus, Rogan, kept up a consistent pace with the cat, skiing as quickly as they could back to Sydney, hoping for whatever medical magic she might still have left to fix Barret and Chester. If they were lucky, they would keep this mystery participant alive long enough to at least get to the bottom of whatever the hell had been going on.

When they arrived back at base, Sydney stood nervously waiting for them. As soon as she saw who the victims were, and who were on their feet, she immediately turned all business and nodded. "Put them on the cots set up here in the clinic." She immediately checked over Barret, confirming that his vest caught both bullets, leaving him bruised and sore, but he would be fine. Then she moved over to the next one.

She stared down at him in shock. "Chester."

He stared up at her, rolled his head ever-so-slightly to the side and whispered, "Will I live, Doc?"

"Yes," she replied, "at least if I have any say in it."

Almost immediately he gripped her arm. "Then don't. Let me go. I'm supposed to be dead anyway."

She blinked as she stared down at him, then looked back over at the others. "I don't think it's quite so easy as that," she replied, "as there are an awful lot of questions."

He nodded. "I have some answers, but I don't have them

all."

"How about starting with why the hell you don't want to live?"

"Because my life after this … will be a shit show." Slowly he gasped for breath and struggled to even speak. "It's time for this to be over."

"I would say it's definitely that time," Amelia stated from the doorway. Joe was beside her. "I think it's way past time, and I sure as hell think you owe this man an apology and an explanation."

Chester looked up at Joe and whispered, "I'm so sorry, man. I'm so sorry."

"Did you kill him?" he asked, his voice harsh. "Did you kill my son?"

Tears in his eyes, Chester slowly nodded. "I didn't mean to," he began. "It was an accident, an accident that I couldn't *not* take advantage of."

"What do you mean, an accident?"

"We were training in the middle East. We were training out in the fields, and, when he went down, and I realized that I'd killed him, I knew I was in trouble, so I changed identities with him. It had always been a plan that my father and I had talked about. I didn't want to be out there, facing the world in wartime," he explained. "I didn't want to see live action. I didn't want to be doing any of it, but I was there, and I couldn't get out of it."

He took a deep breath. "My father kept telling me to walk away, to find a life that I could live with, one that gave me peace instead of torment, but I couldn't. I was stuck in a loop. I was looking for another answer. And then the colonel suggested this. Not killing anybody obviously, but taking a dead man's name. Then the colonel could put me out of the line of fire, and that's what he did."

"So, you took my Chester's name?" Joe asked.

"I took your son's name, even after knowing that I'd killed him accidentally. I probably could have been cleared because Chester stood up when he shouldn't have. He broke cover to save a dog and dodged in front of bullets," he explained. "He had been desperate to save the dog, but, because of our training, … he wasn't supposed to get up, so he ended up getting shot. All kinds of chaos happened, and he got shot for it."

"So, where is my son?" Joe asked, his gaze frozen on Chester.

"It was determined in my briefing that he'd gone missing during that whole scuffle, when in truth I had buried him on the roadside where he died—an act that I have never forgiven myself for, and an act that never gave you any closure. I took his tags, and I left mine with his body," he said. "Then I buried him."

Joe swayed and was caught by Amelia, now both struggling forward, and Mountain rushed to them.

"And for that," Chester said, his tears falling heavily, "I'm so damn sorry. But that's not the worst of it. Then I had to make sure his body could not be identified. So I had to …" He couldn't say more, just wailed.

A shocked silence filled the room.

"I fired aimlessly, I didn't even think about it at the time," he whispered. "He was gone. I couldn't do anything about it, and I didn't want to go down because of it. Maybe it was a chance for me to get moved out," he explained, with a teary face. "He didn't have the rank that I did. He didn't have the pathway that I was on, and I stepped back into anonymity, somebody nobody knew, one who the colonel could then move around. He put me in a different position. … I am so ashamed of what I did, ashamed of walking away from what I was supposed to be doing, ashamed of walking away from what I did to your son, my cousin… and I can't get those visions out of my head. I didn't knowingly kill him, and he did die an honorable death out there but a stupid one." Chester's voice broke with the memories. "I didn't need to deal with it in that way."

Joe stared at him for a long moment. "That's not an honorable death. Nothing is honorable about being shot during training. I hope you rot in hell. His mother died without ever getting any answers. We never had his body to mourn," he bellowed and struggled to get to Chester, but Mountain held him back. "My son was missing in action for years. We got no news, nothing to have closure. We had NOTHING left of him."

Chester nodded. "I shot him and buried him to try and keep some of the buzzards and whatnot away, but I never could find him again. … And you're right. I didn't handle it properly. I didn't do anything that preserved his memory. I took his name and kept on going, and, as soon as I could, I created my new name, something that would be similar but not quite something that would give me trouble. I knew he had friends, people who cared for him."

"And, making it easier for you, paving the way for you, was Elijah and the colonel," Samson noted, with a shake of his head. "Chester, you should have reported the incident. It was friendly fire, with some culpability on the part of Joe's Chester. However, what you did afterward was where you committed various crimes."

Chester faced Joe and said, "I wish I could go back and fix it. I wish I had done the right things and not the rest of it.

I'm sorry, Joe. I really am." Meanwhile Chester gasped in pain, as the blood flowed from his wounds onto the floor all around him. He wouldn't make it. Chester added, "While I'm making my death-bed confessions, everyone should know that Elijah is my father."

Joe stared at him for a long moment. "But you look nothing like the boy I remember."

Chester tried to chuckle, but it came out more as a blood-filled cough. "I grew up, Joe. I think keeping all these secrets inside aged me. I don't know. However, I am truly sorry I didn't do right by you or your son. I wish I could take it all back."

"What do you know about all the killings here?" Mountain asked.

Chester gave a half laugh. "The colonel had a few problems. I was always one of his favorites. … He kind of … held me over Dad all the time, making sure that Chef stayed with him, making sure that Chef followed him into every mission, every battle, every training session. With my father around, the colonel didn't kill anybody," Chester shared, gasping for breath.

"As long as my father continued to look after the colonel in the way that he wanted to be looked after and treated him the way he wanted to be treated, then he would stop killing, but then the brass sent him up here. He's had a ton of experience in places like this, but he did not want to be here. He knew he was on the way out, and it would be ugly, and he didn't want to go the way that they were trying to make him go, and he started to fall to pieces."

Mountain, Sydney, Magnus, Whalen, Nikolai, Egan, Rogan, and Barret all stared at Chester in dead silence.

"At one point in time, I asked my father about it." Chester heaved badly and coughed blood. "The colonel was bad news, and it needed to stop here, but Elijah didn't know how to make it stop. Because the colonel, ... he'd gone off the rail, and he was killing indiscriminately." Chester shook his head. "They were bound by such ugly things, prior killings that I have no knowledge of," he admitted, with a sad smile, "but I had my own debt to pay to the colonel. My father tried hard ... to stop him. He really did."

No one tried to interrupt the flow of information, and so Chester continued. "He gave Amelia supplies. He gave the villagers supplies. Anytime anybody needed anything, ... he was right there for them because, like me, ... Chef couldn't live with the guilt of what had happened. It broke him to know that it was his own nephew who had died in my place, yet ... he would be forced to live without me. Neither one of us wanted to admit what I'd done. The colonel had taken many lives in wartime and in peace. So he didn't care about Elijah and me, doomed to be apart. Lives didn't matter to the colonel."

Joe sniffled, his tears flowing freely now.

"There was no getting away from it. Once you take that corner, you're done. And, with that, always in the back of my father's mind, he kept the colonel from doing more harm all these years, until he came up here, where he slowly unraveled, and there was nothing that could be done to stop it. He kept telling the colonel he had to stop, that this was enough, but the colonel said that I would end up being found out for what I'd done, and then the colonel would have the last laugh because, after all this time, he was the one who knew all about it. Nobody else did, but he was also the one who could pull the strings and who could make it all go away—or it not go away, and we would all go down together."

Chester sighed. "Dad ... struggled with that, and I've never been able to call him *Dad* to his face ever since. Yet that betrayal kept us bonded, and we knew we were both alive, but we both knew that it shouldn't have been that way. Then I found out about Eric, ... that he had somehow found out about the colonel's murders across the pond decades ago. It may have started with just one man, a single man, Nikolai's father, Peter, but it continued on for decades, from what I learned. The colonel was a green kid at the time, ... newly recruited and so excited, and so ... passionate that he lost control, and ... people died."

Chester eyed Nikolai. "Under the guise of training, your father's death was hushed up, and they managed to get it all to go away somehow. Years later the colonel hushed up Joe's son's death and managed to get that to all go away too. I have no knowledge of what killing the colonel did in between those two events, but I'm sure he killed others. He was an unfeeling monster. ... Sometimes it makes you wonder how someone can even do things like this, what kind of sickness within our souls allows it," Chester admitted, tears in his eyes. He gasped several more times.

Then the door opened, and Samson walked back in. Mountain hadn't even realized that Samson had left them. He'd gone to get Elijah.

Elijah walked over to the cot, sat down beside his son and grabbed his hand. "Go now, son, if it's time to go."

His son looked at him, sorrowful, as the life visibly drained from his face. "Why didn't you tell me that you had cancer, Dad? I wish we had more time, but we don't. So you need to tell them everything."

"I will," Elijah vowed, "and I'll pay the price for all this."

"No, no, not at all," Chester argued. "That wasn't you. I did this. And the colonel did the rest."

"But I knew," Elijah said, "and I didn't put a stop to it."

"I'm your son," Chester replied, with a small smile, "and I'm proud to have you as my father. You kept that asshole from killing more people."

"Did I? It seems to me that all I did was make things worse."

"Amelia is alive right now. Nikolai is alive."

"Eric isn't though," Elijah replied, his tears spilling out, "Jerry, Scott, Yegorahn, Ralph, Carl, Kaylan, and many more."

"Yes, we lost them, but Eric was blackmailing the colonel, so I'm not sure that we can give Eric a pass for any of this either," Chester noted. He looked at Sydney and added, "Please tell Helen that she was the love of my life, that she had me wanting to own my mistakes from way back when. And, Dad, I felt you were rebelling against the colonel with your kitchen supplies to those that needed them, which made me want to cut ties with him too. Little did I know that this last favor I would do for him would end my life. … I'm so sorry." Then he gasped several times and fell silent.

Elijah bowed his head and sobbed, as he held his son in his arms, until finally no sign of life was left at all. After a long moment, Elijah looked up and around at all of them. "I didn't have anything to do with any of it, but I knew. Once I found out, I didn't know what to do."

"Turn him in maybe …" Mountain suggested.

"Yes, I should have turned in the colonel. But my son? Was I supposed to turn him in? I couldn't do that, not and still protect the rest of the world from the colonel," he added. "I knew what the colonel had done too. I knew what he was capable of doing, but he wanted me with him, as he was stationed at various bases. We'd been best friends forever, and he couldn't stand the idea that I might turn him in. It was more than he could handle. He always held my son's actions against me. So, I stayed at the colonel's side, and, as long as I stayed, he stayed sane, sober, and controlled, until all three of us—me, my son, and Joe—ended up here at the same time as the colonel."

He took a deep breath and sighed. "Chester and Joe were both here. I knew from that moment on that things would blow up, and they would blow up in an ugly way. Either Joe would get to know Chester and end up digging to find his son or the colonel would pit Joe and Chester against one another, the way the colonel used my son against me. Part of me couldn't wait for the inevitable end, part of me was looking for the release from all these years of betrayal and worry. I tried to save as many as I could here, but the colonel continued to slowly unravel. If I had a good idea of who his target might be, I tried hard to warn them, but who is the one I tell when the colonel of the base is the bad guy?" he asked, with a sad look at the others here. "Given the circumstances, who was supposed to help us with that? There wasn't anybody I could call for help, except one."

"Who did you call, Elijah?" Mountain asked.

He turned and looked at Samson. "Mason."

Several people in the room were shocked, as they turned to look at the man they knew as Samson.

Mason smiled and nodded. "Yeah, I'm Mason. Most of you know *of* me but have never met me in person. I was originally behind the covert investigation, trying to get up here to help out on the ground," he explained. "However, this mission ... was Mountain's. We started as soon as

Teegan went missing, but only recently did Elijah contact me. And he left out a few telling details."

Elijah nodded. "Yeah, but now it doesn't matter because you got them all. It's truly over now," he declared, with a relief so profound that he looked at peace. "And me? I don't have enough life left to even give a damn anymore. Besides, just like my sister-in-law, I won't live long enough to see it."

Sydney looked over at him. "That's why you wouldn't come in to see me. You are dying."

"Yes," he confirmed with a finality. "I already had the diagnosis. I already knew that this would be my last trip. My mistake was telling the colonel. He went off the deep end after that. There was no controlling him. I didn't know how to handle the colonel, how to stop him, and I would be dead soon. … So I called Mason."

"Hence your need to call in the big guns, *huh?*" Mountain noted.

"Yeah, *big guns.* That's partly why I contacted Mason because this was a major problem, with no easy solution," Elijah shared, "because nobody in the military would believe me, even with prior complaints from others. The colonel was trained to kill the enemy in the military. But he took to it too easily, without remorse, without guilt, and it became a personal obsession with him, a side gig, a hobby. I don't know what a shrink would call him—a psychopath, a sociopath, whatever. I just know he was a serial killer who could not be stopped. Not to mention … the colonel would be all sour grapes and giving a million other excuses during any investigation, and he sure as hell wouldn't provide any support, wouldn't give any true answers, and I needed help to keep the colonel in line once I passed on," Elijah explained. He looked over at Mason. "So, thank you."

Mason nodded. "You're welcome, but you know it won't be easy from here on out either."

"No, it won't," Elijah agreed. "I would like to think I could just curl up in a corner and retire, but I doubt that'll happen. I deserve to be court-martialed, but I fear justice will come too late, after I'm gone."

Joe gave a harsh laugh. "How the hell should you be allowed to do that?" he asked, his voice breaking. "After everything, … after my boy is … shot to pieces in some unmarked desert corner … because your son put him there?"

"I know, Joe." Elijah nodded, looking at him sadly. "When was I supposed to tell you? How was I supposed to tell you?"

Mountain couldn't believe it, and yet so much truth had been told tonight that sadly it made way more sense than he ever could have anticipated. He looked over at Mason. "We had stolen drugs and food poisonings and love triangles and stupid bets and Eric's blackmail scheme and the faulty generator issues all the time at the scientists' camp—plus that dead scientist's coded notebook found taped under a chair, which I guess we'll never know what that was about. Still, there were too many suspicious deaths and missing persons, and that serial killer on base had to be found. Little did we know it was the colonel or how many years he had been killing people. Damn, not what we expected at all."

"No, not at all," Mason agreed, with a shrug.

Mountain nodded. "Yet we knew we couldn't go forward without more information. We needed to push this thing to make the killing come to an end." Mountain looked over at Elijah. "I presume you set up the colonel to go after Amelia?"

Elijah nodded. "I did exactly as you suggested. I told the

colonel that Amelia was running and that she already knew, that she recognized him from one of his killing trips, and that's all it took. A few words and he immediately dressed and was gone. So, not only did I allow the military to make all this happen, I also betrayed him."

Mountain shook his head. "That man held you and your son as virtual prisoners, blackmailed you and your son into doing everything the colonel wanted over all these years," Mountain pointed out. "You should have come forward sooner."

"I have no idea what we'll do with any of this," Joe said, looking over at Chef. "Elijah, I'm not sure that I can … It's hard to forgive your part in this, yet … in a way it's also understandable. What your son did, what you did, all you wanted to do was protect him."

Elijah nodded. "I did some things that I'm not proud of, but I never killed anybody. I couldn't, plus that wasn't what I was here to do. If I could kill, if I'd had the stomach for it, … I always knew who deserved it most. I was here to protect people from the colonel, and that was not the easiest thing to do. I spent my life, … all these years, … trying to keep him from killing anybody else. Blackmailing me to keep my son's secret, at the same time the colonel was blackmailing me to keep his own secrets too," Elijah said, with a headshake. "We're a hell of a pair."

He stared down at his son's body, sorrow on his face. Then he got up and leaned over and kissed his boy on the forehead. "There are no easy answers to this one, and I'll be more than happy to join him." He looked over at Joe and added, "I know you'll have a hard time forgiving me for this, but this isn't how I wanted it to go. I didn't know how to get any of us out of it."

Joe sank into the seat beside him. "Jesus Christ, I can't even imagine." He gave a broken laugh. "I spent all this time thinking, hoping, my son was alive somewhere, but really knowing there was no way he could be. Still, I never would have imagined something so convoluted as this."

"That's what happens with just one lie," Elijah noted. "As soon as you lie, as soon as you try to cheat and deceive, the lies multiply and pile up, and you can't ever get out from under them. Once I realized that the colonel would keep killing if I didn't do something more, the only thing I could think to do was to try and stay with him, so that he left everybody alone, and that's what I did. It was my penance."

"At least you had your son."

"I rarely saw my son," Chef noted, "but I knew he was alive, and that was enough. So, yes, in a way, I had my son."

"Yeah, because yours was still breathing," Joe said bitterly. "My boy was killed by your son."

Chef nodded. "Exactly. Mine was alive. Yours wasn't, but I couldn't bring yours back. I won't ask you to forgive me, but maybe you'll understand that life is never easy. ... Bad things do happen to good people. And your Chester? ... I don't know that they'll ever recover his body, yet my boy did go out and make several attempts to find him, but the desert had ... done what the desert does. Sand was everywhere, but the landscape had changed. I'm so sorry for that too." Elijah turned to Mason. "I'm really tired now. Could we possibly call this quits for the moment, and leave me alone for a few minutes to grieve?"

Mason nodded, and, together with the guard, led Elijah to where he had been held before.

Mountain looked over at Amelia, seeing the shock, the sorrow, and the pain on her face, and he nodded. "Not the ending any of us wanted," he murmured.

"No, definitely not," she replied, "but it's almost the ending that had to happen." She looked at Joe and whispered, "I'm so sorry for your loss."

He nodded. "And yet, in a way, this is freedom. This is an answer that I hadn't expected, really didn't want, but at least now I know. So, I'll take it."

Amelia nodded, then turned to Barret and groaned. "Thank you, Barret, for taking bullets for me tonight. I hope you feel better soon. I don't know about the rest of you, but I really need to collapse. I can't feel my legs."

Immediately Mountain was at her side and held her in his arms. "Come on. Let's get you back to your room." As they went out to the hallway, she looked up at him. "Are you okay? That was a lot to digest."

"Oh, I will be, but, yeah, a lot to process. There are still a lot of questions we would like to have answers to—like details regarding my brother—but that probably won't happen."

"No, and I do worry about that. But that is what we have, … and really do we ever get all the answers we want?"

"No, we sure don't," Mountain grumbled. "Sometimes we don't get any of them. As much as that might be seriously depressing to hear," he added, "it is reassuring that we got as much as we have."

"I was wondering that too," she noted. "When you think about it, we already have a lot of the answers. Maybe we can be okay with not having the rest."

As they got to his room, she muttered, "I really need to collapse."

"You lie down. I'll join you in a little bit." He stopped and looked at her closely. "Are you okay without a guard for the first time?"

She laughed. "I'm okay. Honestly I'll crash from the dump of adrenaline that just left me."

"Good enough." He closed the door and immediately headed back to join the pow-wow that would be happening right now. As he walked into the clinic, others were checking up on Mason. Mountain laughed at them. "I guess some people thought they should have recognized you, *huh*?"

Teegan snorted at that. "I kept telling you that something was wrong with him, damn it. Didn't I say that?"

Mason grinned. "Don't feel bad. Those of you who have met me before, you may have never seen me all shaggy and in winter gear," he explained, with a smirk. He grabbed Teegan by the shoulder. "I'm so damn glad you survived that, Teegan. You have no idea how bad I felt, after I was the one who recommended that you come here."

"You're sure as hell guilty for that," Teegan teased, still staring at him, shaking his head at *Samson*. "However, I did come, and this was where I wanted to be."

"Yeah, well, right about now," Sydney shared, as she looked at the group, "I'm thinking that the South Pacific sounds pretty damn good."

Many people seconded that suggestion.

"What do you think will happen now?" Sydney asked, looking over at Mason.

"I don't know," he admitted, with a shrug. "The base will get a new commanding officer and carry on, or, maybe given the mess that we've had these last three months or so, they'll close it down in a few months, whether permanently or part-time. So, you all might have to stay for a little bit longer, if you're willing," he suggested, one eyebrow raised. "I'm sure the brass will check into all the questionable deaths that occurred under the colonel's command over the last twenty or so years."

Sydney shrugged. "I guess that depends on whether anybody else is staying, but, yeah, I signed on for the entire time," she noted, "although I'm a little worried about Amelia."

"Amelia will be fine," Mountain declared. "She doesn't know it yet, but I'm taking her and her dogs down south pretty quick. She's been up here living out in the Arctic tundra for a very long time, and those dogs of hers want their mama back," he said, with a laugh.

"Yeah, I'm not surprised." Sydney smiled.

They looked over at Joe, who even now sat staring off into the distance. "Joe, are you okay?"

"I'm okay," he said, with a sorrowful look around. "I was already thinking it might be time to call it quits, long before all this, and now? … I *know* it's time to call it quits," he stated, with a headshake.

Magnus looked at him with a hopeful expression. "So does that mean … I can have the dogs, right?"

He laughed. "As if I had any chance of keeping them from you anyway," he said, with a smile. "Yes, you can have the two you asked for."

"Hang on a minute," Teegan stated. "He doesn't get any, if I don't get any."

"Every one of you has his favorite sled dog. Thankfully there is no overlap. So let's see who all really wants their dogs," Joe suggested, "and we'll talk about it some more later. Right now, I'll go have a shot of whiskey and commemorate my son's death," he stated, with a careless wave, "and relax, maybe for the first time in a very long time."

Teegan slapped his brother on the back. "Damn it, man,

there's shit no matter where you travel."

Mountain looked at him and nodded. "Isn't that the truth?" Then he shook his head. "In this case though, it's been a whole lot more than I expected."

"Good. I would hate to think you have this shit happening all the time when you are on missions. Where will you take Amelia?"

He laughed. "She probably thinks about going home. I'm not sure how the sled dogs will acclimate, but I would say Australia or the South Pacific, but for now? … Maybe California. … The cabin would do."

At that, Teegan's eyebrows raised. "The cabin sounds like a great idea. Are you guys up for company?"

"Maybe, if you can behave for once," Mountain teased, with a smirk. "What the hell. … Damn right we are up for company. Hell, anybody can come. We all need a chance to celebrate life and not death, … for a change."

M OUNTAIN TURNED OFF the SUV, opened up the back passenger door, and let out all the dogs. Since Amelia's injury, the four dogs were even more protective of her. Thankfully he'd had no issue becoming part of the pack. They milled around excitedly, waiting for Amelia to come out. Then he walked over to the passenger side and opened the door, as he held out his hand.

"When you told me that you were bringing me someplace to recover," she said, looking out the windshield, "I really wasn't thinking here."

"Yet why not?" he asked, with a smile. "Don't knock it until you've had a chance to try it."

She stared out at the ocean in the distance and sighed happily. Before exiting the vehicle, she reached out to cuddle the dogs, who were jumping up anxiously for her to get out. Maybe the smell of the sea added to their exuberance. "I won't knock it. I've always loved open waters."

"Water, whether it's frozen or not," Mountain teased.

She laughed. "Absolutely." She looped her arms around his neck and gave him a hug and a kiss on the cheek. "Pretty damn special place you've got here."

"This …" He pointed to the cabin behind them. "I bought it years ago, as a way to find peace from all the torment and the nastiness that happens in life, particularly with the work that I sometimes do," he shared, with an eye roll. "Don't think this is the stuff I do all the time, but sometimes I do get caught up in these scenarios, and this is where I come to, where I call home afterward, at least for a while."

"What about the rest of the team?" she asked.

"Seems we'll be seeing all of them over the next few days, except Sydney and Magnus. They're staying up there to see this through to the bitter end, and then they'll come home in a couple weeks."

"Will we still be here?" Amelia asked.

He shrugged. "You tell me." He looked at her closely. "I'm up for staying the summer. Personally I think I need it, and so do you."

She smiled, as he picked her up and carried her into the cabin. However, as cabins usually went, this one hardly qualified. She stared, absolutely stunned. "This is freaking amazing," she cried out.

"It's huge, and I wanted the space," he said. "I always figured I would retire here someday."

She nodded. "Well, it's certainly big enough."

"Yeah, it's got four bedrooms and an annex off to the side, if I ever wanted to expand," he noted, with a chuckle. "When it's time to find that place that you can call your own"—he shrugged—"you have to listen to your soul, and my soul told me that this was it."

"Your soul has great taste. I absolutely love it."

He put her gently on her feet, and she looked at him intently. "I am fine, you know?"

He shrugged and nodded. "You might be fine, but you've been badly injured, and I don't want you to get hurt again."

She tapped him gently on the cheek. "Got it, but you also need to realize that I'm fine, that I will be fine, and that I won't get hurt again."

He laughed and said, "Amen to that. Well, come on then, and I'll show you around." Then he gave her a quick tour of the place, ending with the bedrooms. "So your bedroom is here, and mine is right over there."

She shook her head and asked, "Two bedrooms?"

"I didn't want to push you."

She rolled her eyes at that. "Of course you didn't, always the gentleman."

"Come on. Let me show you the yard." They ended up back in the kitchen, where she stepped outside and squealed in delight. "Oh my God, you've got a pool."

"Yeah, I have someone who keeps everything prepped and ready, so it's good to go. Do you want to go for a swim?"

"Oh, hell yes, I do," she declared in delight. "You know the dogs do too."

"Good, I'll meet you there."

And, with that, he headed into his room to get changed. She stared around in shock and joy at the place, then rummaged through her bag, thankful she'd packed a bathing suit for this southern destination holiday, then quickly got changed and stepped outside, heading directly for the water. It would take a while to adjust to being in this location; it was so utterly stunning.

When he joined her in the pool, she was already doing laps – or trying to amongst the dogs' exuberance. He dove in beside her, and, when she finally stopped, he swam alongside her, keeping the same pace.

She splashed him gently. "Always the protector, making sure I don't overdo it."

He shrugged and gave her a big grin. "Hey, when you find something special, you protect it."

She stopped, looked at him, then swiped at the sudden tears in her eyes.

"Whoa, whoa, none of that," he cried out in alarm. He wrapped her up in his arms and held her, still standing in the pool, even while it was well over her head.

But here in his arms, she had absolutely nothing to worry about. She smiled up at him. "You do say the nicest things."

"I mean them too," he stated, with a glance at her. "I'm not one for much flowery speech, but, when you find something that's special"—he gazed into her eyes, holding her tight—"you want to look after it. You want to protect it, and that's what I plan to do."

"I'm fine, you know?" she repeated.

"Good, that's great. Now we can have even more fun."

She laughed. "That sounds good to me too," she murmured, as she nuzzled his chest. "And you can damn-well move me out of that second bedroom." When he looked at her in surprise, she shook her head. "I do not plan on sleeping alone."

His grin flashed, bright and hot. "That's fine with me. I wanted to give you the opportunity to choose."

She shook her head. "Hell no, you were testing me to see if I was ready."

He shrugged. "Hey, I don't want to push you."

She grabbed him by the ears and pulled his head to her, laughing. They kissed, hot and heavy, until he sank under the water, taking her with him. When she came up for air, she was laughing. "You're not pushing, and I am more than ready."

"As in more than ready *now?*" he asked, waggling his eyebrows.

"Absolutely more than ready now," she replied. "Besides, I've never made love in a pool."

"We might have to try it," he suggested, as he looked around, assessing their options.

She chuckled. "We don't really have to test it right this minute."

"No, but it's not a bad idea," he declared, giving her a wink. He moved her over to the shallow end, then lifted her up, so she sat on the side of the pool, and, when his arms came away, her bikini top came with them.

She gasped and then burst out laughing. "Okay, for somebody who *says* he's never made love in a pool, that was a pretty smooth move."

He flashed that audacious grin at her. "Hey, smooth moves are always good." He then lifted her up, and now she was completely nude, sitting there in front of him. He took a step closer, him on the bottom step in the shallow end of the pool and her sitting on the pool's edge. Their heads were now perfectly aligned.

She laughed. "Now that's smart too," she murmured, as she reached out, both arms wrapped around his neck, and kissed him deeply. But his hands were damn busy, caressing, stroking, sliding up and down her body, until she was panting. "Oh, that's deadly. You are freaking deadly."

He nuzzled her gently and whispered, "No, not really. I'm just in love, probably for the first time in my life."

She stared at him in shock, and tears immediately came to her eyes again. When he looked worried, she shook her head. "You say the nicest things."

He lowered his head and kissed her with a tenderness she

didn't think she'd ever felt before. When he finally raised his head again, she had her arms looped about his neck, her thighs wrapped around him, prodding against the erection between them. She smiled and whispered, "A little less talk might be a good idea."

He gave a happy shout, quickly stripped off his suit and, with her still wrapped around his hips, he slipped her off the pool edge, repositioned her ever-so-slightly in the water, and, with her help, he slid right home. She gasped in the pool, the water all around them, the sun shining down, and she realized how absolutely perfect this day was.

With him moving gently, and then not-so-gently, faster and faster, water splashing up around them, she looped her arms tighter around his neck and took over the motions, increasing the waves but also the pace, and by the time her body trembled in response, he had her up against a towel and a floaty, pinned against the wall of the pool, and drove deeper, harder, faster. She came apart in his arms, only to recognize his own climax, and held him as he drove through it.

When he finally groaned and settled up against the pool beside her, she whispered, "See? Even then, instead of my getting hurt by the concrete, you protected me."

He looked at her and smiled gently. "As I said, when you find something special …"

She wrapped her arms around him. "Oh, I agree, damn special," she murmured, "I sure hope we can stay here for a while, and the dogs appear to be totally okay with it." Matter of fact, they were still in the pool, splashing on the far side, playing and generally having a grand old time. She loved it, absolutely loved it.

"I figured we could use this as a base," Mountain explained, "and come and go as we need to, maybe make it our permanent home. We'll see how many times you decide to spend some time up north, and we can sort it all out."

She nodded. "I do want to go back to the village again."

"We did say goodbye."

"But briefly," she pointed out.

"Yes, briefly." He grinned. "Honestly, I think they're all relieved that we're gone at this point."

She laughed. "You could be right. It was not the easiest training session for them to witness."

"No, it sure wasn't," he murmured, as he nuzzled her neck, and then whispered against her, "You ready to go again?"

He sat her on a lawn chair and drifted downward, his tongue, his hands, his mouth, all driving her wild with the sensations, the sun above them, and the joy that flowed through her. By the time they'd made love several more times, her body sang with joy and fatigue. "I don't think I ever want to leave."

"And you don't have to," he said. "We'll make this a home base for both of us. I meant that."

She looked over at him. "There's a strong sound of permanence to that."

"I sure hope so." He tilted her chin up and whispered, with excitement on his face, "Amelia, will you marry me?" She looked at him with a stunned expression. "Will you be my wife in all things, my comfort, my joy, my partner, … in good times and bad?"

She was dumbfounded.

"Will you stay by my side because I can't think of anything more precious than spending every last moment of every last day together with you."

With tears in her eyes, she threw her arms around his neck and cried out, "Absolutely yes."

EPILOGUE

T HE PLANE TOUCHED down in a controlled smooth movement, hardly jarring the few passengers seated inside. A gorgeous blue sky was outside, a typical sunny California day.

Mason and several other men from the Shadow Recon team waited for the plane to come to a full stop. When it finally stopped rolling, Mason grabbed his bags, tired, happy, but somewhat sad.

As answers went, the ones the team had found in the Arctic training base hadn't been the easiest. At the core was fear and self-preservation. Such common human failings and, in this one case, one with massive consequences, as individually the men involved had slid deeper and deeper into their lies and deceit.

The fact that Elijah had reached out and had contacted Mason directly would help his case but not enough, though it sounded as if the cancer would likely take him pretty damn quickly anyway. Still, he wanted to answer as many questions about as many cases as he could, so some families could find some closure.

Mason wanted that too. Families were still suffering, as they looked for answers to the deaths of their loved ones. Deaths that were meaningless, senseless, and all the more painful for the betrayal by these men, who should have supported their military brethren, not taking them down, not making them victims.

When the back door to the plane opened, and Mason walked out onto the tarmac, he held up a hand to shield his eyes, wishing he'd brought his sunglasses with him because it was a bright sunny day. Tesla was planning to pick him up, and they would spend a few days together, before he headed back to the office, his field mission over.

He headed for the main hangar, falling in behind the other men. He had places to go too, but chances were good that Tesla would be here somewhere, waiting. And she never did what he expected of her. She was her own person, a special soul, and he was blessed every day to come home to her.

Hearing a shout off to the side, he turned and caught sight of her, hopping out of the Jeep and rushing toward him, her pregnant belly bouncing lightly with every step.

Mason grinned and laughed, as she opened her arms and raced toward him. He dropped his bag and raced in her direction.

He hadn't made it ten steps when an odd *ping* hit his head, and he was stopped in his tracks, a slow paralysis taking over his body. He stared at his beloved wife, watching her confusion, then her horror, followed then by her scream that seemed ripped from her very soul.

Mason's knees buckled, even as he recognized the red flow covering him was his blood. He collapsed to the asphalt beneath him, and the world around him went black and silent, … as he was sucked into the murky darkness.

This concludes Book 8 of Shadow Recon: Mountain.

Read about Jasper: Man Down, Book 1

Man Down: Jasper (Book #1)

There is no greater motive than bloodlust, DNA, and revenge, all mixed up in a cocktail of hatred …

Jasper, who witnessed Mason go down, is all-in on the investigation. He's on top of the current team, almost pushing out of the way his distrust of everyone around them. Tesla, his cousin, trusts him to get to the bottom of this and fast.

ER nurse Amber isn't on Mason's team but knows something major is happening. The hospital is overwhelmed with men, asking for updates on Mason's condition. A few look as if they belong—and a couple don't. Taking some discreet photos of those in question, she sends them to Jasper and starts a cascading chain of events. None of it good.

Jasper is soon sidelined from hunting down Mason's shooter with keeping Amber safe, when she's targeted next. He must keep them both safe, … even as the investigation heats up and gets even uglier.

Find Book 1 here!
To find out more visit Dale Mayer's website.
https://geni.us/DMSMDJasper

Author's Note

Thank you for reading Mountain: Shadow Recon, Book 8! If you enjoyed the book, please take a moment and leave a short review.

Dear reader,

I love to hear from readers, and you can contact me at my website: www.dalemayer.com or at my Facebook author page. To be informed of new releases and special offers, sign up for my newsletter or follow me on BookBub. And if you are interested in joining Dale Mayer's Reader Group, here is the Facebook sign up page.
http://geni.us/DaleMayerFBGroup

Cheers,
Dale Mayer

About the Author

Dale Mayer is a *USA Today* best-selling author, best known for her SEALs military romances, her Psychic Visions series, and her Lovely Lethal Garden cozy series. Her contemporary romances are raw and full of passion and emotion (Broken But … Mending, Hathaway House series). Her thrillers will keep you guessing (Kate Morgan, By Death series), and her romantic comedies will keep you giggling (*It's a Dog's Life*, a stand-alone novella; and the Broken Protocols series, starring Charming Marvin, the cat).

Dale honors the stories that come to her—and some of them are crazy, break all the rules and cross multiple genres!

To go with her fiction, she also writes nonfiction in many different fields, with books available on résumé writing, companion gardening, and the US mortgage system. All her books are available in print and ebook format.

Connect with Dale Mayer Online

Dale's Website – www.dalemayer.com
Twitter – @DaleMayer
Facebook Page – geni.us/DaleMayerFBFanPage
Facebook Group – geni.us/DaleMayerFBGroup
BookBub – geni.us/DaleMayerBookbub
Instagram – geni.us/DaleMayerInstagram
Goodreads – geni.us/DaleMayerGoodreads
Newsletter – geni.us/DaleNews